To Katie,
Enjoy

Angels Club

COURTNEY VAIL & SANDRA J. HOWELL

COURTNEY VAIL & SANDRA J. HOWELL

WEST RIDGE FARM PUBLISHING
Hampden, Massachusetts

Published by West Ridge Farm Publishing in Massachusetts
Cover Design: Amy Rooney
Cover Photo: Bigstock

Publisher's Note: This novel is a work of fiction. Names, characters, places and incidents are either products of the author's imagination or used fictitiously. All characters are fictional, and any similarity to people living or dead is purely coincidental.

ISBN-13: 978-0984558254 (West Ridge Farm Publishing)
ISBN-10: 098455825X

Printed in the United States of America

 For the outcasts & dreamers

1

Horses are my passion and have been for all of the eleven years I've been dancing on this earth. I love, love, love them. I pretty much live and breathe for them, as anyone with the stomach to handle my little sister's tornado mess can tell with one glance in our shared room. Horse figurines and posters are everywhere. So the major —and I'm talking *major*—bug out of Emily's green eyes as I looked down at her in her wheelchair from my perch on the rust-colored saddle of my favorite horse, Ginger, had me shaking my head as though I couldn't solve a riddle. What in the world! How could she not want to kiss the face off of this loveable cupcake? Ginger's the smallest, sweetest horse on the whole farm with eyes like chocolate pudding. Emily got the prize pick right here. She's the most requested horse, especially by the younger kids because she's not too tall or peppy.

The jittery ten-year-old with cerebral palsy had already

spent two Saturdays here at Sunnybrook Therapeutic
Horse Farm, grooming the horses, feeding them carrots,
getting to know all *nine* of them so she could choose her
favorite of the lot. If she couldn't find the courage to let
her red curls bounce around for a bit during a little ME-
led stroll, she *should* be ready to at least *sit* on Ginger.
Come on. It's no big deal. Saddle up, *chica*! It's not like
you'll be galloping through the fields solo. Emily looked
like Merida from *Brave*. She just needed to find some
inner bravery herself.

My neck itched from impatience. I scratched it and
gazed around the massive indoor riding ring. All the other
kids were already being led around on their horses and
were clamoring with cheer. Even those with balance
issues who had instructors walking alongside were riding
proud like cowboys.

In the four months I've been volunteering here, Emily's
definitely not the first skittish person I've seen, but I
honestly can't remember anyone taking so long to get up
on a horse.

"I'm scared, Jacinda," she said, her voice creaking. Her
fingers twisted together in a tight ball.

"It's no big deal. Watch." As I picked up the reins, I
clucked and prodded Ginger with a light touch of my leg
to urge her around the ring one more time. Hopefully, this
would show Emily her gentle nature and reassure her that
she was a super easy horse to ride.

When Ginger stopped in front of her and blew through
her nose, the timid girl hesitantly reached up and stroked
the mare's silky mane. Emily seemed to warm up to her as

the mare stood quietly waiting. Even Ginger wanted to get on with this and show her she wasn't some big, bad beast to fear. I actually think this mare, or, *all* the horses here really, understood the importance of the job they have because they stayed so quiet and patient around the kids.

"See, Em? It's super fun and easy peasy. Ginger's such a sweetie pie. I told you she's the best one for you. Are you ready to climb up?" I swung off the saddle and jumped down onto the dirt floor beside her. "Don't worry. I'll be leading the whole time, and Miss Jane'll be right beside you, holding you steady. So there's nothing to be afraid of. I know you can be brave and that you'll love it once you're up there."

"Maybe. I want to. I just can't stop shaking." She clenched her eyes for a moment and scrunched her hot pink shirt as she nodded. Her eyes were as big as saucers when she looked back at me. "Okay, Jacinda. I think I'm ready. If kids much younger than me can do it, I have to at least *try* this time."

"That's the spirit! Hey, Miss Jane." I called and waved the instructor over to help Emily get up. "She's still nervous, but she's ready to mount."

Miss Jane hustled over and Miss Carol too because Emily would probably need a double-lift.

Emily has gotten some leg mobility back since her last surgery but climbing the steps and lifting her leg over was going to be tricky. They helped her gingerly up a three-step mounting block and then hoisted her up onto the horse.

I was so proud of Ginger, standing so still and calm, like

she was aware of the nervousness of the rider now straddling her back.

Miss Carol left to help another boy, and Miss Jane and I aimed to make sure Emily was comfortable. We adjusted the stirrups so Emily's brown boots with the pink lightning bolts could slide in. "See? It's okay, Emily," Miss Jane said. "I knew you could do it."

Emily puffed up a red curl that fell in front of her eyes. It flopped right back down to where it was, but she didn't budge her hand from the saddle horn to fix it. She was holding on so tight, her arm muscles strained and her knuckles turned white. "Wow! Oh my word! This is so high up in the air. I'm used to being *much* closer to the ground." She swayed a little to get a feel for the leather seat beneath her and looked all around the ground below her.

"It just takes some getting used to," I said. "But you'll rock it in no time." I swept the stubborn curl out of her eyes and tucked it behind her ear, then picked the reins up for her to hold. "Let go of the saddle horn and take hold the reins. You'll be okay."

Emily let out huffy breaths.

Miss Jane said, "Are you gonna just sit here for today, Emily? Is this enough? That's fine too. You don't *have* to ride."

"Ride a little bit. Come on. You can do it, Em," I said, taking the lead line in hand. "See how sweet this girl is? Touch her between the ears. She's such a cuddle monster. She loves that. Neck hugs too."

Emily freed at least one hand from the horn. She leaned

forward and softly stroked the black hair between Ginger's ears. "She *is* so soft."

"I know. I love the way they feel."

She took the reins from me but quickly brought them down in her fist to return to the double grip.

Miss Jane said to Emily, "Are you ready to take a few steps? I'll stay with you until you feel comfortable and I know you can ride securely on your own. That won't be until the next week or two, probably. But when I see you have good balance, you won't need me to walk alongside."

Emily sat up, let out a slow breath, and nodded.

Miss Jane gave me a thumb's up. "Okay, Jacinda, let's just walk a little bit and see how Emily feels."

I snickered quietly because she was still trying to crush the horn. I led Ginger to the right five steps and looked back to make sure Emily wasn't gonna pass out on me. Seeing she was fine, I turned my attention back to the horse. "Ginger, you're such a good girl." I stroked her face. "I have special treats for you back at the barn. A nice, shiny apple. And, guess what! I found your favorite brush."

Miss Jane said to Emily, "Far enough? Wanna stop?"

I stopped and looked back to find a huge smile instead of a rectangle cringe. I guess that meant Em forgot all about being scared. A desire to stop wasn't likely.

Even as she was still hanging onto the horn for dear life, she cried, "No, no, I want to go a little more. It's not so bad."

"Okay, Jacinda." Miss Jane said, motioning to keep going. "Let's do a walk around."

I started leading Ginger around the ring and scratched her neck to tell her how proud I was of her.

Emily was so thrilled, she started giggling, and that filled my heart with fuzzy-mitten warmth.

"Yeah, Jacinda. You were right! This *is* a lot of fun. Can we do three more laps? I think I can do it myself, Miss Jane."

"No, no. Not quite yet. I'm glad you're feeling good, but I need to stay with you to make sure you can sit up on your own *without* holding onto the horn and you demonstrate good balance. Maybe next time. We'll see."

"Oh, goodie. My tummy's still somersaulting, but this isn't as scary as I thought. I feel like such a baby for freaking out."

"No biggie," I said. "We all get scared sometimes." *Right. Sometimes? Try, every day.* But I bet anyone walking in *my* cowgirl boots would have butterflies dancing in their belly too. I just can't, for my life, make any friends at my new school. My parents divorced two years ago, and my mom, sister, and I lived with Abuela Rosa, the sweetest grandma in the universe, until she died this past May. Now we live in a five-room ranch right down the road from Sunnybrook with a massive kitchen that seems like it was accidentally put in the wrong home. Friends flock to my sassy six-year-old sister who does crazy things like stuffing my shoes with grape jelly, while I, the *nice* one, always have to eat lunch alone. It's embarrassing and so unfair. As if I didn't have enough on my humble-pie plate, meanies are always making me feel like a slug. I haven't been punched or anything *yet*, but my neck is always prickly and my shoulders tight. I've had almost a month to scribble names on my birthday party list, but it only has *Kat*, my out-of-school BFF, on it. But, when I'm with horses, or Kat McKinley—whose family owns Sunnybrook—or my family, even though it's a little broken, none of that matters. I come alive.

Aaahh. *This* is the life! Did I mention I love horses? Even this slow walking rang as music to my ears. Their soft steps on dirt or steady clops on cement filled me with glee. Ginger's smooth walk that was only very gently rocking its rider made me smile so big. It was amazing to me how these horses instinctively knew to be extra gentle and easy with the kids who came for therapy. Not that they suddenly went crazy or buck-wild or anything with more experienced riders, but there was a definite difference in stride and demeanor.

Sunshine flooded my heart and made me beam when Emily completed all three circles without flipping out or begging to come down. She laughed and chattered like a cartoon bird the whole time. That was it for her lesson today, and she did awesome. I was so happy she found the courage to get up there and that she had fun, just like I knew. Ginger did awesome too. Love her to bits!

Miss Jane helped Emily slide off Ginger and into her wheelchair, then took the lead line from me and led the brown horse to another boy for his lesson.

At the end of the day, that sweetie'll definitely get the treats I promised her.

Emily was still chirping with excitement when we exited the barn.

As I helped her wheelchair over roots in the ground, the rumble of a diesel truck and the clacking of a horse trailer fired an arrow of delight into my chest. I looked over my shoulder and shrieked when I spotted the towed treasure trove being backed up to an empty paddock. "Oh my goodness! They're back!" Kat had gone with her dad to pick up a new prize. I bopped Emily's upper arm with the back of my hand. "Come on! Let's go check out the new horse Kat and her dad snagged today! I am so psyched, you just don't even know. I bet it's a beauty. I'm sure it is. I mean, every horse is beautiful in its own way, right?"

She nodded, but I could tell she wasn't as absolutely certain of that fact as me.

Emily's chair was motorized, and she zipped over there, keeping pace with my lanky legs, which took up almost two-thirds my body. Clapping her hands and hooting like an owl, Emily was clearly just as thrilled as I was to meet the new addition to the farm. She'd turned horse lover in one brief flash of fearlessness. We were soul sisters now.

As Mr. McKinley opened the trailer, I jumped up and down, squealing, then I went around to greet Kat and discuss their hot find.

Kat flung the truck door open. She was so excited to see me, she slipped getting out and nearly fell on her knees. But I caught her and saved her skin from the sure scrapes the jagged gravel would've given her. It must've been a long, hot day for them because Kat's blond hair was a wreck. Frizzy pieces stuck out of her hair tie, and it was starting to poof and fuzz out on top. She always pulled her long, bushy hair back in a tie or braided it. Otherwise, it looked like a squirrel's nest, especially whenever she sweated. Even though I can usually understand her speed talk, today all her words about the rescue farm jumbled together like a ball of tangled Christmas lights.

She's as horse-crazy as I am, but that's pretty much where our common ground ends. We look nothing alike. She's a bitty peanut, currently sporting braces. She *hates* her metal mouth and envies my perfect smile. And although I can be very nutty, I'm no little nut. I'm a totem pole with caramel skin, brown eyes, and long, dark brown, pin-straight hair. Because of my height and summer-grown curves, people often think I'm fourteen. She hates being a short pretzel stick, and I hate being tall and older-looking, especially in my new school of pipsqueaks. I hate the way boys are always looking at me and the stares and whistles I get from older ones when I'm at the mall or whatever. I tend to keep my head down and eyes lowered and walk fast so I don't have to look at anyone. Mami's always reminding me to hold my shoulders back and be proud of the way I look. She says I'm unique, but I feel like an ogre. And Papi, whom I stay with on Tuesdays and Wednesdays, teases me with, "What are you looking for? Pennies? Lift your head up, *Bella*—which means 'beautiful' in Spanish—so you don't fall. If you don't look forward, you might miss something." Papi always calls me *Bella*. Ugh. Not even.

Kat was jumping up and down and finally said something that didn't spaz out my brain. "Wait 'til you see what we brought home. You won't believe it! We got *two*."

Her dad, dressed in his typical flannel shirt, jeans, and John Deer cap was out of the truck, and I jumped as high as I could to get a better look. I saw the rump of a black horse and the rump of a smaller, big-question-mark horse. The shorter one looked to be predominantly white, but it was so hard to tell. I'd never seen a horse this scuzzy, like it had been jerked out of a mud bath. Both were whinnying and stomping their hooves, anxious to get out into the fresh air.

Mr. McKinley walked around to the back of the trailer and slid the bolt back. Now I could see them better. Oh my gosh! I gasped. Horse trailers are large with tall sidewalls separating each horse. I could already tell the black one on the right resembled Black Beauty. Mr. M hopped up and in, unhooked the tie from the black horse, and clipped a lead line on its halter. Then, he slowly backed it out and down onto the ground.

Kat took the lead line from him and brought the eye-popping stunner to the side of the trailer while her dad returned for the white ... well, *kinda* white ... horse.

"Wow. You're so unbelievably pretty," I said, patting Blackie's neck and stroking his sleek back. He felt so silky. "You take my breath away. Can't wait to ride you."

Kat said, "I know. Isn't he gorgimous? Wait 'til you get a better look at the river-rat one. What a major yuckfest."

"Aw, no sir. The poor thing. Is it a mare?"

"Mmm hmm."

"She just needs better care than what she obviously got, that's all." My eyes stung and I almost sobbed when Mr. M. turned her around and I saw her boney sides and flanks. She was stomach-twistingly scrawny and there wasn't a place on her that wasn't filthy. Large spots of mud looked to be plastered on her side, and a bushy, tangled mane, crusted with dirt, hung over both sides of her neck. A long forelock dangled over her eyes and almost covered the long, curled, white eyelashes. I'd never seen such a sad-looking creature in my life. She stood quietly next to Mr. McKinley. He handed me the lead line, and I walked the pathetic thing to the side of the trailer next to Kat.

She walked beside me, gentle as a lamb.

"Whoa," I said, bringing her to a halt, while I waited for Mr. M to tell me where to take her. I spoke quietly to her. "There you go, sweetie. You're out now. It'll be okay. You can frolic in the fields, eat to your heart's content, and just relax and take it easy." She smelled like wormy rain puddles, strong horse urine, and manure, but I didn't care. I continued to talk softly to her and she appreciated my attention and nuzzled me with her soft nose. I reached up and pushed some of the mane away from her eyes. That was when I got my first good look in her deep, mesmerizing pools of hot fudge. Her large eyes pulled me right into her soul and we made a connection. Oh my gosh! I fell in love in that moment. I just ... *melted*. I ran my hand under her mane and scratched her neck. She moved her head against my hand, confirming that we'd just become friends for life and telling me she wanted more scratches. She must be pretty itchy with all the mud and whatnot matted on her.

Emily, not as comfy or thrilled around the new equines now that they were out and right in front of us, just sat there staring at the scraggly one. She didn't say anything, but she was probably grossed out. Her eyes, big as cookies, volleyed from horse to horse, and I could see her mentally comparing them. Although she didn't know as much about horses as Kat and me, it was evident the one on my line had traveled a very rough road. Compassion and concern bloomed in her eyes.

Kat looked over at me as I rubbed the white horse's side. "What a freakish thing, huh? She doesn't even fit in here at all."

Yeah, sadly, I had to agree. This disheveled sweetheart looked nothing like the other horses on the farm, which were always groomed and kept clean. We hosed them down when they got too hot and sweaty, and when needed, we rubbed horse shampoo on them to get them extra clean. We loved giving them a sudsy bath. The horses here were all healthy and in excellent shape. I wondered what happened to this pitiful beast and how she ended up so thin and dirty. That kind of lax care and neglect made me so mad and it was something Mr. McKinley would never stand for. So it surprised me he took this one home too. Maybe he couldn't resist. Her eyes did plead for help and love. The castoff looked like it understood what we were saying and stood quietly by my side with its head down. It did nothing. It didn't even budge when a fly buzzed around its tail. I bet she truly felt as defeated as she looked and acted. Having a spotless, black prize beside her only made her look that much worse by comparison. "Kat, don't say that. Seriously. I think she feels bad when she hears those words."

"Oh get real. As much as I love horses more than most of America, I know they aren't like people."

"I don't know. Maybe they're more like us than we think. They all have emotions and vivid and varied personalities, that's for sure. And this poor thing is bummed out beyond belief."

"Well, I can't be bothered to mind her *feelings*. Sassy's my full responsibility now."

"Sassy's her *own* horse," I told Emily. "You only saw her briefly in the stall, but wait 'til you see her in broad daylight. She's so gorgeous, you might cry. She's the color of what's known in the horse world as grulla. Her body is slate gray and she has the cutest star snip on her forehead. Her legs, tail and fetlocks are black, and her mane too, but her hair has thin golden highlights that shimmer in the sun. A large dorsal stripe runs down her back and horizontal stripes are on her legs, kind of like a zebra, so she's definitely one eye-catcher. She stands out around here. But *this* poor thing..." I stroked the white horse's neck, "what's gonna happen to her? She's an eye-catcher for an entirely different reason."

"Dad says we aren't keeping her. We'll fatten her up and sell her. The man we scored the black gelding from offered the white rescue for free, and dad felt so bad when he saw her, he couldn't say no."

Just then, Mrs. McKinley emerged from the house and hustled over to us. She smelled like cinnamon apples and had an apron tied around her waist. She wiped her hands on it and ran her hand through her short, blond curls. "What's with *two*, Jack? Thought you were bringing home one. We don't need *another* riding horse. Why would you bring home another one? This white one looks in really rough shape. I can't even tell what breed it is. It'll need a visit from the vet and look at its feet. It sure hasn't had a trim in a long time."

I looked down at the hooves. They were cracked and nicked. She was right.

"Couldn't just leave it there," Mr. M said.

"Why not? What are *we* gonna do with her? She's a bag of bones and will be a costly burden more than anything. And what's with the thick wavy hair? I've never seen anything like it." She looked at me and asked, "Have you?" like I was the horse expert here, even though Kat knows a ton more than me. I liked that she had enough confidence in me to ask, but I really couldn't help. I was just as buzzy-brained as she was.

"Nope," I said, shaking my head and shrugging. "I don't know what breed she is either."

Jack said, "The fellow, Rick Mason, who I purchased the gelding from, rescued this one from animal control this morning. The owner had fallen ill and was placed in a long-term care facility. Neighbors tried to take care of the corralled horse the best they could for almost a month, but they were forced to make a call, and it was taken away. Rick was going to rehab her but offered her to us. He thought with some fattening up and cleaning, we could sell her to get money for the program."

"Look it, Jack. While I appreciate the sentiment, we're already pressed for time. You *know* our fundraiser's just around the corner and getting her ready for sale'll be a huge time zapper for us. And in the end, she'll just be uprooted again."

"Let's talk about this later. For now, let's just get her settled in, fed and watered."

Mrs. M huffed slowly and rubbed her temple with the heel of her hand, as if already feeling the exhaustion of the job just by looking at the mare. "Okay, you girls, walk 'em both to the back barn and put 'em in the two empty stalls. Water them and throw them some hay. We'll look at 'em later. When you're done, can you finish cleaning the stalls in the main barn?"

"Yes, ma'am." Without even really thinking it through, a sense of urgency forced me to say, "Um, Mrs. M? If you wouldn't mind, can I take her on as a project horse? You said she'd be a huge time zapper for you, time that you don't have. *I* can take care of her, clean her up, as well as train her to ride and follow commands. Problem solved. Pretty please?"

She sighed with her lips scrunched, hopefully seriously considering it.

Even though I knew *that* was gonna be a monstrous job, I was so quick to volunteer because I honestly felt like I was the only one who truly *got* this horse and saw her potential. Everyone else just saw a headache and a big mess. She was counting on me, and I couldn't let her down. "Maybe she'll end up being an excellent addition to the program. You think?"

"Oh, I really don't think we can use her here, sweetie," she mewed like I was so dumb and silly for even suggesting it.

I know I stayed back in third, but I am *not* dumb! This horse just needs a chance to show what she's got! A strong determination to change everyone's mind bubbled up in my mind.

"She's just so different," she said with a sneer. "But, go ahead, Jacinda. If you want to take her on to make her good enough for *sale*, I don't mind, but she'll be your responsibility. It'll take some time for her to regain her health. Just to get some fat on her will take time. We'll have the vet check her out first, and then have her hooves trimmed. It'll be a lot of work for you, and you'll have to commit to put in the time and effort. You ready for that?"

I looked over at Mr. M, and he winked at me. "Oh, yes. I can do it. I'll come at least twice a week after school to work with her. And you know I'm already here on weekends. Mami and Papi won't mind, as long as I keep up with my studies and get my work done."

Hmm. Yeah. I *sounded* all gleeful and sure of myself, but a boulder of anxiety fell into my gut. I clutched my belly as I looked over my new project from snarly, muddy mane to unkempt hooves. Can *I* actually help this poor horse? Me? I think so, but it looked like it had been to the worst pit and back.

Ugh. I hope I'm actually up for the job and not in way over my head.

2

The tacked-on chores made it a long day of work for Kat and me. Emily helped out with some too. She especially loved opening the gate to let some of the horses out to play and graze.

After brushing Ginger and giving her the shiny apple I promised her, which she thanked me for with a sweet nuzzle, I dashed back to the barn holding the disheveled mare that was now my very own big project. Under all that dirt, I was pretty sure she was all white, but she could have some special markings too, which would be cool.

Kat and Em were still with her, talking about her current state of yuck. Man, I really wished they'd give her a break. *She* couldn't help it, and this condition was only temporary.

"Awww," I whined, rubbing her between the ears on her matted head. "Poor thing. Besides neglect, I wonder what other nightmares she's been through. It'll be dark soon. We don't have time to beautify her today. We'll have to tackle that huge task tomorrow."

"Beautify her? Humph. Doubt that's even possible," Kat said, punctuated by a sneer.

"Sure it is. Have some faith, in her *and* in us. With a good wash, or a couple, and some grooming, she'll at least look halfway decent, and definitely smell way better."

Kat said, "I don't know. She's a walking disaster."

The horse drooped her head low again and slowly munched up a blade of hay.

My heart ached for her. I really think she knows exactly what we're saying. Or most of it. "She may be a walking disaster right now, but she has the most beautiful eyes ever. Did ya see 'em? They're so gorgeous, they pull me right in. Not only do they hold so much emotion, look at those curly lashes. They're like dainty butterflies."

"What, do they *speeeeak* to you?" Kat mocked with a wiggly dance.

"Yes, they do, as a matter of fact. And they say, 'I'm better than this. Don't judge me.'"

"Hey, can I help you clean her up tomorrow? Please?" Emily cried with one clap and pleading eyes.

I looked at Kat for her opinion and she shrugged that she didn't care. "Yeah, sure," I said, "*if* your mom doesn't mind you being here all day. Giving her a bath'll be a lofty job. We'll want to see if she's been handled too. We can definitely use more helping hands."

"No, my mom'll be thrilled I found something to do on my own. She's always wanting me to make more friends."

I cringed with a lop-sided sneer because my mom was

always nagging me about the same thing, but Emily's frown and head droop said she'd read my expression all wrong.

"You don't want to be friends?" she creaked. "I thought ... I thought..." Two giant tears rapidly formed and rolled down her cheeks in uneven streams. I didn't think tears could form and melt that fast. "You two are the *only* kids who've looked me in the eye all week. Whether I'm on my crutches or in a wheelchair, people ignore me and act like they don't see me at all." Her voice started breaking like glass. "So, I was hoping, I mean, I just assumed ..."

"No! We're friends, we're friends!" I cried, cutting her off and waving my hands. "Oh my gosh. Please don't cry. Of course we can be friends. I don't have a single friend in school, not one. So when I did that whole face scrunch thing, I was thinking about how my mom's always badgering me too, *not* that I didn't want to be your friend. Sorry." I looked at Kat with insistent eyes and a finger wave to back me up.

Kat nodded and rubbed Emily's shoulder. "Yeah, of course we can be friends. We're *always* looking for more friends, Em. So don't flip."

"Never. Trust me. You wouldn't wanna see *my* cartwheels," Emily said, smiling big at her own joke and wiping her eyelids.

We all fell into a fit of laughter at that. I was glad she had a sense of humor about her condition.

"Why would people not wanna look at you though?" Kat asked. "I don't get it. You're so crazy-adorable. Wish my curls were glossy like yours. All *I* have is a pompom."

Emily bit her lip and her eyes got shinier. "Well, my mom says people feel sad or awkward when they see me in a wheelchair, or my funny walk, and they don't want to offend me by staring or saying the wrong thing. But I'd much rather get a stare or a blunt question than the pretending-I-don't-see-you thing I usually get."

"That's so awful," I said, rubbing her upper arm. "Not to mention rude."

"It so is!" Kat cried. "See? That's why I like to be loud and sarcastic. Being short puts me below the eye level of most, but my big mouth makes me impossible to miss or ignore. You should try talking to people first, to break the ice and show off your inner sparkle. Jacinda and I can help you with that."

"I'd *love* that. Thanks. Uh, I'm so relieved." Emily patted her chest with both hands. "I thought I was getting ditched again."

"Nah. We squabble sometimes, but we never ditch. Right, Kat?"

"Yep."

Emily wiped the lingering wet ribbons off her face, and the white mare, with her head turned, saw that and circled around and moseyed up to her. She rubbed against Emily's face and licked her.

"Oh my goodness! What a lovey-dovey girl we have here," I cried, patting our new equine friend. "She's so sweet like Ginger and Sassy. Even after all the neglect and whatever else she's been through, she's trying to cheer you up and comfort you, Em. See? I told you there are some special horses who are just naturally angels."

Emily curled her fingers under her nose. "Uck, although she stinks like she's lived with a gang of wild hogs, that's what you should call her." She giggled at the horse's eyelash tickle. She stroked the horse's head. But, not ready for a slimy face-to-face smooch, she tried to shoo it back with her fingers.

Kat nudged the horse away from Em's face.

"Call her what?" I said.

"Angel."

"Nah, I was thinking, Dirt Digger myself," Kat said with a sneer, brushing the mare's filth off her fingers. "It's so much more fitting."

"We are not calling her Dirt Digger," I spat.

Kat cracked up. "How about Toad then?"

"No," I growled. "I really like Angel. It's a good name for her. Thanks for suggesting it, Em. I bet if we can get her looking up to her natural glory, she really will look like an angel, or the swift-footed carrier of one. Maybe she'll even look like a unicorn." I scratched the mare under the chin and neck, and she lifted her head, telling me, *more, more, more.*

"Doubt that, but you can call her whatever you want," Kat said. "She's *your* horse."

"She's not *mine* ... just my sweet-as-candy project horse."

"I really like '*Angel*' as her name. It's perfect." Emily beamed.

"Perfect? Ha," Kat shrilled. "She's so far from heavenly,

even demons are pinching their noses and are racing away to find some sulfur to sniff. I'm not even lying when I say that's *the* ugliest, most wretched horse I've ever seen in my twelve years of existence."

"She's *not* ugly," I said, rubbing her back. "She just … needs some sprucing and primping."

"Or a lit match."

"Hey, cut it out!" I whacked Kat's arm. "That's not even funny."

"You *know* I'm kidding! I hate to see any creatures in distress."

"You're twelve?" Emily cried. "Never would'a guessed that. You look younger than me."

"Yeah, tell me about it," Kat groaned, crossing her arms. "I was asked to play Baby Jesus in the church play last Christmas, but they changed their minds when they saw my tinsel teeth." She grinned wide and goofy to show them off.

Emily bowled over, laughing and clutching her stomach.

"Apparently, Jesus doesn't *really* sparkle."

Emily kept on laughing.

"Shut up," I bellowed. "She's exaggerating. She does that. Like, constantly."

Emily looked at Kat and then at me with a crinkled nose of confusion. "Last week, Jacinda, you said you were *almost* twelve and live right down the road. You don't go to the same school?"

I shook my head with my lips curled in. "Nope. Annoyingly, I was held back in third, so I'm only in fifth now, which puts me embarrassingly in the same new school as my six-year-old sister, Tia. Being in a sea of mostly ten-year-olds, and younger, only makes me stand out like a freakish, lumbering giant."

"You're not *that* tall."

"I'm 5'4", and most of the kids stand beneath my shoulders."

"We're all pretty much freaks then," Emily said. "We've got a gimp, a tree, a shortcake and a smelly disaster of a horse."

"Hey! Don't call yourself a gimp!" I yelled.

"Oh joy," Kat muttered. "We're like the Island of Misfit Toys. We should form our own club."

I could tell by her sarcastic tone she was joking, but I nodded, loving the idea. "Yeah. We should."

"I was *joking*!" she screeched with laughter.

"I know. But it's a fab idea. I'm just not sure what our club should be about, but we're all unique and talented in some way. So, I'm sure, combined, we can all put our hashtagable awesomeness to good use. Once we get Angel looking parade-worthy, we should, at the very least, try to find Angel's previous owner. It's not his fault he was hospitalized or whatever. We can send him pictures and some 'Hope You Are Feeling Better' cards. I really do hope he's doing much better."

"Me too. You have a really big heart, Jacinda," Emily said with a smile. "I like that. It's a great idea, one *I* should have thought of because I've certainly seen my share of hospitals. I know, just know, that man will love it. You were very patient with me, waiting for me to get up on the horse. You pushed me in exactly the way I needed without making me feel like a baby chicken. Hey! Maybe we should just do nice things for people and try to help whoever we can, especially other freaks like us."

"Exactly." I nodded with my smile sliding into an even bigger crescent moon. "The world is full of meanies. Each one of us here has been beaten down or ignored, so let's be the opposite and try to make the world a little brighter. Instead of being more monsters in the mix, we can be angels instead."

Emily's bright smile said she adored the concept we came up with, and I took Kat's nod of approval and shoulder shrug as good enough to be in too.

"Awesome!" I crossed my arms with a bounce of pride and elation. It was as ragtag and pitiful as this horse, and very tiny, but I had myself a club! An *Angels* Club.

3

It was Sunday, thank heavens. Cleanup time! Angel had all my thoughts lassoed in a big red bow, and my heart too. I couldn't wait to wash the gunk and stink off of her and see what she really looked like. I didn't even have to wait for the loud, pulsing buzz of my alarm. I beat the sunrise, and by 7:00, I was showered, dressed, and stuffed with two slices of peanut butter toast that I'd folded and wolfed down.

Sunnybrook Farm was only two miles from my home, which was the best thing ever. Not only did I love the exercise of biking or even jogging there, but the destination was heaven-on-earth.

I hopped on my bike and pedaled there as fast as I could. Part of the way was up hill, so I was out of breath by the time I was crunching up the long, rocky driveway and zipping over to the barn where Angel was stabled. I don't think I'd ever gotten here quicker than today because this was the first time I felt winded from the short ride over. I propped my bike against the barn's wooden-plank side and ran in to get started. I set my bike bag on a wooden bench in the corner.

I knew the horses were fed and waiting to be turned out. Mrs. McKinley was always in the barns by 6 a.m. She liked to, "Get a move on," as she says, "as soon as the rooster crows."

Kat was already there waiting for me. She had Sassy on the crossties. Even though Sassy was Kat's horse, she was also used in the therapeutic program.

Kat gobbled up every equine magazine she could get her hands on and researched horses online with the intensity of a forensic scientist. I was more of a book reader and collector of all things horse. We always exchanged new info we found, especially cool tidbits about the different breeds. Between us, we held a mountain of knowledge. Most of the horses here were considered grade, which means mixed-breed. To earn a home at the McKinley's farm, a horse only needed to have a pleasant nature. *Usually* calm, steady and sane won them a home here.

I flipped my gaze from Kat's gleaming beauty to Angel in the stall. No wonder Kat and Mrs. M looked at her with an, "Ugh." Angel had the sweetness to live here, but she looked absolutely nothing like the others. "Are you ready to turn Sassy out so we can start on Angel?"

"Yup, she's ready. Aren't you, Sassy?" Kat ran her hand down the side of her prize, and I could see the love in her eyes as she spoke to her. Sassy nuzzled her hand, looking for the peppermint Kat usually gave her in the mornings. Sassy took the sweet candy from her palm with her soft lips. I could only imagine Angel being this beautiful when she was all cleaned up.

Kat unclipped Sassy from the crossties and I walked to Angel's stall. She stood patiently with her shaggy head over the wooden rail. A day of eating good hay and grain didn't make any difference. She still looked way too thin. Visible hip bones were not what you wanted to see on a horse. I didn't realize until I felt my heart sink in this moment that I'd been hoping for magic.

Running my hand down her head, I said, "What a darling you are. Don't worry. We're gonna get you good and cleaned up, okay?" I twisted her tangled mane together and she looked at me with her dark brown eyes. They were so soft and trusting. "Okay, girl, it's *your* turn. Sure hope you like baths and that you don't flip out on me." I picked up a halter and lead line off the wall next to her stall and opened the gate. Angel calmly stood there. Although it was possible *cruelty* made her so passive and easy, I really think it was just her personality. We didn't name her Angel for nothin'! "I'm gonna take you out to the wash stall for a good scrub, and pretty soon, everyone'll see how beautiful you are."

Angel stood still while I put her halter on and clipped the lead line to it.

Kat came back in the barn after turning Sassy out and walked over to us. "Wow, she looks no better today."

"She *will* once we give her a bath."

"Or *five*," Kat groaned.

Before I had a chance to speak up for Angel or ask where Emily was, I heard the whirr of her wheelchair. "Awesome! Em's here. Now we can get to work."

I think Angel heard it too. She turned her head to look.

"Wait!" Em hollered. "I brought a carrot for Angel. Is it okay to give it to her now?"

Not at all alarmed by the zippy speed or sound of the wheelchair, nor Emily's loud shout, Angel bobbed her head, like, *yeah, you'd better gimme that carrot.*

Leaving to get her mom, Kat waved and said, "Hi," to Em as she rolled down the aisle and stopped beside Angel.

"Sure. Go ahead," I said. "She'd love it *and* she clearly wants it too. That's her nod of appreciation."

The mare lowered her head right next to Emily and gently took the carrot from her hand. Munching the raw veggie, Angel rubbed the side of her nose against Emily's arm, another gesture of thanksgiving for the treat. It was clear Angel remembered her and loved her to bits already.

My eyes tingled with salty rain puddles. I sighed and muttered a whine of protest to myself, "But Angel's too heart-lovely for a heave-ho. She so belongs here." I dabbed the outer corners of my eyes before tears fell.

"Oh, she tickles," Emily laughed.

I sniffed. "She likes you." I was thrilled to see Angel giving Emily courage.

Angel stayed near her new redheaded friend, shaking her head a little like she was trying to nudge out a nose scratch.

Seeing their interaction made me all the more certain Angel would make the *perfect* therapy horse. But how could I convince Mrs. M? All she saw was a funny-looking reject. "Ready to help, Em?"

"Sure am. Just lead the way and let me know what to do."

"Grab the bottles of shampoo and conditioner from my bike bag, will ya?" I shouted to her as I walked Angel down the aisle of the barn.

"Kay." Emily quickly found them in my bag and wheeled after us toward the wash stall.

"Thanks! You can stick 'em in your basket for now."

Angel was behaving so well, I couldn't believe it. I could tell this mare had some good training under her belt. Someone had worked with her, but she'd just fallen into a world of neglect.

Sunnybrook Farm had a great wash stall on the side of the barn with a cement floor. Two large posts with hitching rings to clip the halters to were set in the ground, and rails were on either side to keep the horse in one place. "See this hose, Em? It sprays warm water. If the horse stays calm, we can walk in beside it to hose it down. But with an antsy horse, we wash it from outside the rails. It's important to always talk to a horse if you're anywhere near its body or in its strike zone, so it knows where you are and won't get spooked. Soft talking also soothes them. I like to think they enjoy the things I say to them too."

"I'm sure they do," she said with a big smile.

Yesterday Mrs. M told me to only walk Angel into the wash stall and see if she'd stand quietly at the crossties and said to do no more until she checked on us. After all, this shaggy beast hadn't had a bath in weeks, maybe months, and it was impossible to know how she'd react. Sure enough, Angel walked in without battle, and I clipped her to the crossties. "Wow, you're such a good girl."

"Does she just stand there for the hosing?" asked Emily. "Or does she get dunked in some kind of horse pool too?

I snickered but stuffed it before it turned into a hyena's cackle. Emily was a newbie here. She'd never seen a wash stall, or a horse having a bath for that matter.

"What's so funny?" Emily's sad face said it all.

Oh no! She thought I was making fun of her. "Nothing," I rushed out. "I forgot you never gave a horse a bath. There's no pool. Just the hose action. The image of what you said made me laugh."

"Oh, when you said, 'a bath', I pictured a pool with a walk-in ramp."

I nodded. "Yeah, I can see how you'd think that. No, we only use the hose. But now, because Angel is new and we're not sure how she'll react, we have to wait for Mrs. M."

"What can *I* do to help?"

"You can hand me the shampoo and conditioner when we need them."

"Okay. Cool."

Kat came out through the barn with her mom.

"Hi, Mrs. M," I said with a finger-wiggle wave. All the kids called her Mrs. M.

"Morning, Jacinda," she replied in her cheery voice. "Your horse looks content and happy there. She led all right for you?"

"Yes, ma'am. She was a peach." Angel was standing

quietly, not moving a muscle. She didn't even twitch her tail when a fly landed on her rump.

"Well, she's either an exceptional mare, or she's been through this before, although you can't tell by looking at her." Mrs. M walked all around Angel, checking her out. "Okay, Kat, turn on the hose and let's see how it goes."

Kat turned the faucet on and let it run a minute for the warm water to spill out. Angel didn't look any more wide-eyed or stiffen up at the rush.

Mrs. M had brought her box with large sponges, horse shampoo, and a sweat scraper, and she set it down.

"I brought my own shampoo and conditioner," I said. "They're in Emily's basket. She's gonna hand them to me when we need them."

"Great," Mrs. M said. "I'm so glad to see you getting more comfortable around the horses, Em."

"I love them now! What's that giant squeegee thing for?" Emily asked, pointing.

"It's called a sweat scraper," I told her. "It's used to run along the horse's body to wipe off extra water after hosing them down."

"Why can't they just shake the water off like dogs?"

I smiled. "Well, dogs can be dried with a towel. A horse is too big and the water soaks under their hair and onto their hide. It's easier to use the scraper. I'll show you how we do it. It'll be too high for you to try, but you can watch."

"Wow. I have so much to learn. I feel like such a moron."

"You're not, don't worry. Kat and I'll teach you. Soon, you'll be experts, just like us."

That brought a big smile to her face.

Mrs. M started hosing Angel down. She began on her hooves then moved up to her ankle and her leg. Angel, my perfect girl, didn't budge and looked like she was enjoying every minute. I'm sure the warm water was like a huge relief and a big treat over the brown plaster gunking up her whole body. When Mrs. M hosed her side, Angel remained steady. "Well, girls, I think you can take it from here. She's doing great. I'll watch for today to be sure she's okay. You've never had to wash a horse this caked-up and nasty-looking before, and I wanna be here in case she gets startled. She looks to be taking the hosing fine though. She'll definitely need two sudsy baths to get that coat clean."

I took the hose from Mrs. M and worked it over Angel, doing one side, then the other.

Emily's wide eyes and goofy smile said she was fascinated by the bathing process.

A brown river streamed off of Angel. It must've felt so good.

Once we had her soaked, Mrs. M said, "I'd start the shampoo at her legs and see how she takes that. Her fetlocks are so dirty. Interesting how long they are. If I didn't know better, I'd say she has Draft horse in her."

"Draft?" Emily asked. "Like the ones in the beer commercials? I know I don't know much about horses, but she looks a *lot* smaller to me. Does drinking the beer help them get that big?"

I curled my lips in to stifle a laugh.

Kat stressed, "Draft is a *class* of horses. Draft horses, yes, like the Clydesdales in Budweiser commercials, are usually large and stocky. But they don't drink beer." Kat stopped speaking and scrunched her lips to catch her composure. I could tell she was so ready to crack up. "They're used for pulling carriages or work. I love watching them in horse pull competitions."

"You're right, Kat," said Mrs. M. "She isn't as tall as a typical Draft. It's frustrating me that I can't figure out her breed. She's so unusual. But we'll tape her and at least know how tall she is."

"What! You're gonna wrap her up in tape?" Emily cried in shock.

"No." Kat chimed in again to explain to Emily what we were talking about. "Taping is a way to measure height. Here, I'll show ya." She walked to Angel's front legs and rested her hand where her back and neck met. "Look here, Em. This is called the withers, the top of her shoulder blade. So, we put a special tape measure that has hands and inches on it and we measure from the ground up to the withers to know how tall a horse is."

"What's a hand?"

I huffed and just kept on hosing Angel down, leaving Kat to answer Emily. It was cool Emily was interested now, but her countless questions were frustrating me when I was trying to concentrate on washing a horse that currently looked more like a mud monster.

"A hand is a measurement that comes from a long time ago. Back then, they didn't have a ruler or something to measure a horse, so they used their hand in the same way we use the tape. They placed one hand above the other and counted. Each hand is four inches."

"I'm gonna research *everything* about horses," Emily said. "I was only taking riding lessons to make my mom happy, but now, I love horses and want to learn all about them. They're so cool."

"See? I knew you'd warm up. I'm ready for the shampoo, Em," I said. Angel was as soaked as possible, but the water was still running brown as I held the hose on her. "Whew! She's gonna need a ton of suds to blast off this mess."

"No kidding," Kat scoffed. "Too bad it doesn't come in a cement truck."

Cracking up, Emily took the shampoo from her basket and handed it to me. "Oh my goodness. That would be so funny if it did. Can you imagine calling in the order?"

"Hilarious." I snickered. "Usually, we dilute shampoo in a bucket of water, but for this bath, we need it straight-up." When I poured in on her fetlocks first, as Mrs. M suggested, Angel began to dance a little. "Oh no! She probably doesn't like the cool, slimy feel."

Without hesitation, and much to my shock, Emily wheeled around to get closer to Angel's head and began speaking quietly to her.

Mrs. M launched forward with her hand out to stop her, but Angel settled down in an instant and put her head down to greet her friend. Mrs. M eased back and let the beauty happen.

Emily pet her nose over the rail. "It's okay, girl. They're

just working to get you nice and clean. You'll feel so much better with all that mud gone. It'll go faster if you're still and quiet like before."

I was ecstatic seeing how Angel stopped fidgeting in a flash so we could get the shampoo in.

Her hair was thicker than any horse's we'd ever bathed, so dirt clung to her with Thor's grip.

It was clear as raindrops to me that Angel loved Emily. I'm sure everyone knew it too.

I tried pouring on more shampoo, and this time, Angel stood quietly listening to Em's every word about how beautiful she was. "It worked! Good job, Em!"

Kat filled a bucket for me to squeeze the large sponge for rinsing.

"Hand me the rubber curry comb too," I said, "so I can really work this in."

She started scrubbing Angel's fetlocks and legs.

"I came to help," Emily said. "Can I stand against the rail and continue to hose down the front of her while you two are shampooing her back? She's still got a lot of dirt there."

"I don't know, Emily," Mrs. M said kind of groaning. "Got the strength for that? Your surgery was just six weeks ago. Your mom told me last week, you couldn't spend as much time on crutches as you'd like to."

"Yeah, but that was *last* week. I've been doing awesome. Jacinda said you wash the horses from outside the rails if they're grumpy. No, you didn't say grumpy. What'd you say?"

"Antsy."

"Yeah, antsy." She looked at her with pleading eyes and her fingers twisted together. "I can do it, Mrs. M. I know I can."

"Okay, Emily," Mrs. M said. "Give it a shot. I'll be right here if you have any problems."

She gripped the rail with both hands to help herself out of her chair. She looked pretty steady as she braced her torso against the metal bar. Being closer to Angel also looked to be giving her strength.

I didn't realize I was holding my breath in nervousness until my lungs had a feeling of relief when I exhaled. But I worried for nothing.

Her smile was like a half moon when she took the hose from me and began washing Angel with us. She looked like a pro with the hose. She kept talking to Angel, which helped the horse stay super relaxed.

As Mrs. M supervised us with her arms crossed, I could tell she was anxious to get back to her work when she quickly glanced at her watch.

We piled on shampoo and rubbed it in. Large soapy suds kept flowing over Angel and small bubbles floated above her into the air. A big, iridescent globe popped on Emily's nose, but her giggle of surprise told me she didn't even see it coming because she was too busy looking into Angel's eyes.

"I want to get her back, sides, and legs finished before we start on her mane and tail," I said.

Angel stepped back when I put shampoo on her upper back. "Whoa," I said, and she stood again. "Well, she can follow verbal commands," I stated, even though I already knew. I wanted Mrs. M to be impressed. "Aside from the little jig, she's been so great through all of this." I knew it was a lot for her because bathing her was no picnic, but I could tell she was really enjoying the attention and sensations, with all the hands working on her. It had probably been ages since she'd gotten the spa treatment.

Kat and I kept talking to her, along with Emily, while we soaped her up so Angel would know where we were. Kat lifted the bucket and dunked Angel's tail into it.

Still, Angel did nothing bad. Okay, maybe a little something bad. She twitched her tail and it flicked soapy, sludgy water on Kat's face.

Kat screeched and cried, "Ugh, so nasty!" She smeared the water off her face.

Emily giggled. "Haha. She got you good."

"Whatever," Kat said smugly. "No mints or carrots for you from me, Rat Face. Sassy never does this. When I'm giving her a bath, she's like one of those frozen guards at Buckingham Palace. You *know*, Jacinda, as soon we put Angel out, she's just gonna roll in the dirt."

"Horses do that?" Emily asked.

"Yep." I held out my hand to take the hose from her. "Thanks, Em. That was great, and you were a big help. We'll shampoo the front, and then hose her all down."

She handed me the hose and inched back down into her purple cushioned seat. Her smile was still almost touching her ears.

When we got Angel good and sudsy in front too, Mrs. M said, "Rinse time. It'll be good to get the first layer of dirt off and see what we've got."

Kat and I hosed the filthy suds off and stepped back for a better look. Now it was even more evident how skinny she was. Her thick hair was slicked down and her hips looked bonier than ever.

"Wow, she looks so pathetic," Kat said, "like I could knock her over with a lollipop in my hand."

"Yeah," I said. "But at least she's … *whiter.*"

"Okay, girls, give her another quick, soapy wash and finish up her mane and tail. Then, that's it for today. She's had enough and we need to stop on a good note."

"Uh, thank God," Kat said, with an exaggerated groan. "My arms feel like cooked spaghetti."

We shampooed her body again and the sudsy water did rinse off much cleaner this time.

Her mane was thick and kinky and cocooned in dirt, so it would be the hardest thing to wash. I slowly poured the water from the hose onto it. She tossed her head, splashing us, and I moved the hose a little to see if she would settle down. "Shh, I know you don't like the water so close to your nose and ears, but it's okay, girl. You need this." She soon calmed, and I poured some shampoo onto my hand and sponge and began rubbing the suds through her mane. Dirt ran down onto her side. Once again, Angel surprised me with the trust she had. "See? Told ya she understands. Look how swiftly she relaxed with a few soothing words." I really began scrubbing, and Kat held the hose there to wash away the dirt that kept on streaming. Then, I moved to her head and forelock. I stood in front of her. Scratching the side of her nose, I told her she looked beautiful then picked up the long tangled forelock and rubbed it between my hands. I kept the water and suds from her eyes with a cloth.

Kat came up front to help me. She rubbed a sponge over the front of Angel's face.

The white was so pretty. Her ears were filled with curls. I'd never seen that on a horse. "Hey! Check out her ears, Kat, all the curls in there. How adorbs is that!" I took a soft wet cloth and cleaned the inside. I couldn't see in well because of all the curls, but I could feel the dirt and scabs caused by bugs and her rubbing her ears. I carefully washed as much as I could. "Mrs. M? Got any type of lotion I can rub in her ears? It looks like all of Whoville was slain in there."

Kat laughed.

"Sure, dear." Mrs. M came over and took a look and sent Kat back to the barn for some soothing salve to put in her ears.

"Emily, hand me the conditioner please," I said.

I took the bottle from her outstretched hand and poured some onto my hands then rubbed it all through Angel's mane to make it soft. She only needed one more run of the hose over her whole body, mane and tail. I kept it on her until suds stopped dripping. I turned off the faucet and set the hose down. Uh, finally, we were finished and she looked stunningly beautiful. Well, at least I thought so. I put salve in her ears, and Kat and I used the sweat scraper to pull off the excess water.

We were drenched, but it had been worth it. Angel looked like a million bucks. Okay, maybe fifty bucks, but at least she no longer looked like a mud troll.

Mrs. M left the barn to work on other chores.

Without the mud weighing it down, Angel's mane began to spring up and look ringletty like I'd twirled sections around my fingers. "Wow. Check it out, Kat!" I cried excitedly, pulling her by the arm to get closer to its head. "Do you think this is an American Curly Horse? With those white eye lashes, the thicker coat, and the curly mane and tail? Aren't those *Curly* traits?"

"Yes! You're right. Oh my goodness! I've never seen one in person before," she chirped. Okay. *Now* she was excited about my project horse. Her eyes gleamed with joy.

I beamed. Angel had been an angel through it all, even with strangers bathing her, but with all these curls and the white everywhere, when she fully dries, I know she'll look more like a unicorn.

Though that was a job and nine halves, Angel didn't feel like a project to me at all. I loved her so so much. When I looked into her eyes, all I could see was *friend*. And I knew Emily felt the same. Maybe Kat too.

But cement filled my heart and lungs because she was like none of the horses here. I needed to find a way to convince Mrs. M that she belonged here too. Because there was no way on earth I could let her go now. Friends *always* gotta stick together.

4

My mom was making burgers and barbeque chicken on the grill for supper, so I invited Kat and Emily to eat and discuss Angels Club. We were all sprawled out on my bed. Resting on my pretzeled legs was a notepad with—*big surprise!*—a horse on the cover, and I had my purple feather pen in hand ready to scrawl words of hope.

We'd already been here five minutes, and Emily was still looking around, turning this way and that, to take in the entirety of my homemade horse poster wallpaper. The paint in here was an icky, blah orange, like it was mixed with way too much tan, so even my sister Tia, who liked to be my habitual road block and personal imp, didn't mind my passion bleeding into her side of the room and whooshing around back towards mine.

"How many more posters do you think you'll need for the whole room to be a total horse cave?" Emily asked. She was holding and petting the unicorn my

Abuela Rosa gave me when I was a baby. It's my most prized possession.

"Maybe ten for the wall. And I need two skinny ones to put over the door and closet. Sunnybrook Therapeutic has an annual fundraiser and vendor exhibit coming up mid-October, so I can probably score some hot pics there."

"Oooh, I'd love to go to that," Emily said.

"Don't worry, you probably will," Kat said. "There's a rider's showcase where kids in the program can show off their skills."

"Ohmygosh! No way! Will I have to leap over hurdles?" she cried and slapped her chest.

Kat touched her arm and laughed, "No, silly. Just ride. You can do that fine, especially with several weeks to practice."

She relaxed with a huge sigh. "Uh, phew. I would've super-glued my hands to the horn and my butt to the saddle if that were the case."

"Why don't we just write down our talents to get some direction," I said. "Whatcha good at, Em?"

She just shrugged. "Not much of anything. I can win a science fair, but that's not exactly gonna help anybody."

"Well, Kat can draw and paint. I can … reach top shelves. Woo hoo!"

Kat swatted me. "Cut it out. It's a thing she hides, but Jacinda can sing. Did you know that?"

"Nope." Emily shook her head with a big smile on her face. "Come on. Sing something. Know any Taylor Swift?"

"Noooo. Uh uh. No way. I don't like to sing in public."

"We're *not* public," Emily said. "We're just ... two mop tops."

"Yeah, Jace. We're two circus clowns," Kat said. "Goofy Poofy and Carrot Top. Siiiiiing."

They laughed, and I shook my head vehemently and waved my hands. "Nope. Not gonna happen."

"What about on tape?" Emily asked, getting serious. "When my baby cousin was born premature, the music therapists in the neo-natal unit were always looking for soft music and kid-sung lullabies. Most kid's music is chipper and poppy, but they like soothing stuff."

"Now *that* I would do. I love, love, love that idea!" I said, getting up and twirling. "Can you see the heart balloons lifting from my mind? Can you? Can you?" I crashed down and groaned though. They both laughed at my exuberance. "But, ugh, I'm not much of a lyricist. To be special and angelic, we'd need to create our *own* music. Do either of you write poetry or anything that I can turn into songs? The lines would definitely inspire melodies."

They both shook their heads.

"Rats," I said, putting a big question mark by it.

Just then, Tia came bouncing in. "Hi. Can I play with you guys?"

"No! Get out!" I cried, launching off the bed. "We're not *playing*. We have important business matters to discuss."

"What business matters?" She giggled. "You don't have a business."

"No, but I have a club."

"Can I be in it?"

"No. It's only for non-annoying girls, which you, unfortunately, are not."

"Hmph. Well, *pollo loco*, don't wanna be in your lame club anyway." She stomped out and slammed the door behind her.

"You should let her in," Emily chided me. "We should be open to anybody who wants to help."

"She doesn't want to help. She only wants to get in my way. She just called me 'crazy chicken'."

"Can you at least think about it?"

"Maybe," I spat. "I'll *think* about it, okay? Can we get back to business now?" I hummed, trying to figure out how to best use Kat's drawing skills. "Hey. Here's something we can do, Kat. In addition to sending one to Angel's former owner, we can make get-well cards for kid's hospitals and maybe some pictures and thank you picture-notes for deployed military. I just don't know how to go about doing that." I wrote that on our list with a big question mark.

"Oh, I can find out online!" Emily rushed in with. "I'm really good at sniffing things out."

"You are? See? *That* is what I'm talking about," I said, giving her arm a light slap. I scribbled out the question mark, because I felt confident she'd find out how. "*Those* things. It's something you do all the time, so you don't really think of it as a talent, but it can be used to help people. You can teach seniors at the senior center to use computers and find things on the internet, for instance."

She beamed, obviously loving that idea.

"So, do we want to do things in secret?" I asked.

Emily laughed and said, "Maybe *some* things in secret. But what am I supposed to do as a techie helper? Wear a mask?"

We all cracked up at that image.

"Hey, I know," Emily said. "A young mom, like eighteen or nineteen, lives near me in the center of town. Her baby is one and a half. She doesn't have a car, and the bus doesn't come out this far, so she does all her shopping every Tuesday and Friday at that tiny Brickman's Market where the prices are jacked. She pulls a red wagon. Do you think we could pool money and give it to her? If we could give her like, I don't know, seventy-five dollars or something, it would at least help her out for one week."

"Seventy-five dollars?" I cried. "It may as well be a million!"

"I know it's a lot. I just feel so bad for her. We can leave a little gift box with the manager at the store. He will do me that favor. And we can watch from the pizza shop across the street."

I looked at my bureau with a sneer. I had thirty dollars in broken bills, hidden from Tia, that I'd saved up to get some horse posters at the show. That mom definitely needed it more than me. Posters weren't a necessity like food. I cringed and said, "Errr, I have almost half of that. And there's a bag of cans on the back porch. I can recycle those and get a couple more bucks."

"You do?" Emily screeched. "That's awesome! I have some money in my bureau. Maybe twelve dollars. I'm sure we can find change and stuff."

"You and Kat can dig around and let me know how

much money you find. I can't do it Tuesday because my dad works weekends and I stay with him on Tuesday and Wednesday. That's the only time he has to see me. But, Friday would work. Hopefully, we can get a good amount."

They both nodded in agreement.

"Got a cellphone, Em?" I asked.

"Yep."

"Call me early in the week to let me know it's *on* and how much money you find. I really want to give her seventy-five, at least, if we can."

"Yeah, me too," Emily said.

"I totally love the ideas we're coming up with," Kat said. "Should we have a calling card when we help someone? I can make a logo, and we can get those perforated business cards and print out notes that say something like, '*Angels smiled on you today. Go be an angel too.*' That way, we inspire people to act themselves and make the world brighter along with us. Don't ya think?"

Kat's usually a little cynical, so I was surprised that caramel-filled Hershey's Kiss came out of her. It was brilliant! "Yeah! Definitely," I cried. "That's a great idea. I love it."

"I do too," Emily said. "We'd be melting hearts and taking care of the meanies, one by one. Soon we'll outshine them by millions."

"All that's needed is some motivation to act," I said. "Wow! I feel so powerful and warm-fuzzy inside right now. Don't you?"

They nodded emphatically.

We all started laughing and shouting in victory cheers, "We're Angels, woooo!"

For now, I felt like Queen of the World.

Tomorrow, however, was another storybook nightmare, in which the only thing I'd be ruling was Slugville … my very own town of one.

5

On the rumbly grumbly ride to school, my fun thoughts about how amazing Angel will look once she's gotten some more meat on her dissolved when a baby chick hatched in my throat. Rats and bats! There went all my strength again, zapped in a flash as soon as the bus door folded open.

I huffed and rubbed my suddenly achy neck before I groaned and tugged my bag into the aisle. My nerves buzzed like a fluorescent light as I dragged myself off the golden chariot with the hopes that I'd survive the jabs from gladiators and lions. I mentally had to cheer on my legs to get them to move.

I sneered, then took deep breaths to try to calm my racing heart as I passed over the cement welcome mat that screamed, "Stop! Go back! Go back!" instead of, "Hi. Come in and stay for a while." I'm pretty sure rocks lived above the double doors at my school entrance with the sole purpose of leaping onto my shoulders every day. Then, at the end of the day, they'd climb off, giggling, and jump up and down on the roof in celebration for successfully giving Jacinda Gonzalez yet another bulky day. I looked up at the arch window over the door and grumbled under my breath as I passed through. Yep. Sure enough, the familiar load of terror found me as soon as my sneakers started squeaking on the tile and the scent of paste hit my nose along with vinegar cleaner. I could feel myself slouching as I rushed to get to homeroom without snagging the attention of any she-devils.

But good thing I listened to Papi's advice about looking up and forward. The sight of a new, tan-toned girl in a Red Sox shirt stopped my pink Chucks cold. I *know* she's new because there are only five other Latinos in the whole school. Knowing these halls just got another pinch of zesty spice, I did a tiny jig that I hoped no one saw and shook my fists excitedly. Another thing that *guaranteed* me she was new was she appeared to be lost. She kept looking at the piece of paper in her hand, then at the doors or hall signs, then back at the paper. She pivoted, shook her head, and huffed in annoyance. She was clearly in need of a helper. And that would be me! Luckily, *I* spotted her first over some mean troll demanding she pay for passage with chunks of her soul or all of her lunch money.

"*Hola, chica,*" I chirped, skipping up to her. I should never skip. Ever! It's lame. Plus, I probably look like a drunk giraffe. "I'm Jacinda. Need help finding your class?"

"Ugh, nice assumption that I speak Spanish."

"It's 'hi, girl'," I snapped. "Even any kid who watches *Sesame Street* knows that one."

"Never saw it. Don't care. Leave me alone."

"You've never seen it?" I cried in astonishment.

"Nope. Muppets annoy me. Leave me alone. The last thing I wanna do is form some piñata sisterhood here." She sneered like I smelled bad and started walking away from me.

"Hey!" I cried. "What's your problem? I was just trying to be nice!" *Whatever. Go on struggling with a search-and-find rather than getting help from me. I don't care.*

"Ewww. *Dos* Tacos," Victory Miles said when she turned the corner with her best friend, Posh.

I groaned. I was trying to give New Girl a friendlier welcome than the wormy words I knew would come flying at her at some point today. From Tory or Misty or ... or what was his name again? Bruce? Yeah, Bruce the Brute. Oh well.

With her path now blocked, New Girl stopped in her tracks.

"Yuck," Tory said. "Just hearing your half-English voices made breakfast spoil in my stomach." She's my arch nemesis. She hates me, and her name already spells out who the winner is, so I don't even bother fighting. What's the point? I think she has everyone too afraid to talk to me.

I scowled at her.

Tory clasped New Girl's wrist before she could get away. "Listen up, Taco Thing Two. Let me give you a little tip, as a favor, because you're new. You don't wanna be caught dead talking to the Jolly Green Giant over there.

Her last school was condemned. Who even knows what germs you'll catch."

Jolly Green Giant? My heart sank as I clutched my green, soccer ball shirt. Okay, now I knew *green* was definitely *not* a color for me.

New Girl turned back to scowl and huff loudly at me, like the insults were all *my* fault.

I had *nada* to do with Tory's bad attitude. She's just that way. She's the farthest thing from an angel possible without veering into criminal acts.

New Girl jerked her arm free and rushed away, leaving me all alone with the glaring trolls.

Without the stares of steel they were sporting now, these two looked like mini models, perfection in every way, unlike gangly me. They were so beautiful.

Tory's shiny brown locks waved perfectly around her oval face and created a swirly frame for vibrant, blue eyes. And Posh was even more beautiful with dark skin, hazel eyes, and long hair that was sectioned up into about a hundred braids. I think Victory thinks of Posh as her sidekick, but Posh out-classes her by miles. Haha, *miles*. She's the queen of cool accessories, nails, and shoes, and always looks runway-ready. Today, her braids were all twisted back in a knot with long Oriental pins, which complemented her shiny, button-collared Japanese shirt with colorful birds and winding cherry blossom limbs. I wish she'd break out from Tory's thumb and be nice whenever she wants to be because she's really only ever mean to me when her BFF is around. But today, she let Tory's under-the-border comments stand alone.

They left me, thank goodness, but the damage was already done.

As the day went on, I itched to toss this shirt in the trash. Tomorrow, I'll bring a spare in case I misfire in my fashion choices again.

After lunch, I got a call from Emily. Hearing her voice and enthusiasm perked me up, but we didn't even have sixty dollars among us to give to the mom, so that made my heart heavy. "I really wanna give that young mom at *least* seventy-five like you said. Once I recycle the cans, that'll only give us, at most, three more dollars, which brings us to fifty-seven, including Kat's money. I'm gonna check with the office here and see if we can do a bake sale. However, I don't bake well. Do you?"

"Nah, not really. I'm good at stirring and delumpifying though."

"Bummer. Okay. I'll get back to you. Bye, Em. Enjoy the rest of your day." I stuck my phone back in my locker. The clang on metal reverberated when I slammed it in my rush to run to the office for a minute. I almost crashed into New Girl when I pivoted. "Sorry. Wasn't paying attention."

"What are ya doing?" she asked softly.

"Not your business." I went to veer around her but she grabbed my arm.

"Sounds like you were trying to collect money for a young mom. Who?"

I shrugged. "Ah, I have no idea."

She shook her head and cried, "Wait! You don't know? How do you not know?"

"She's on my club's list of people to help. And, *nooo*, it's not a piñata club. We just do good deeds. Or, that's what we hope to do. This mom's our first target."

"Wow. That sounds really … cool. Can I be in your club?"

I pitched back on one foot and stuck my thumbs in my jean pockets. "I don't know," I said, suspicious. "We're a gang of misfits. Can you handle that? And hold off on the snarky attitude while you're at it?"

She looked down at her sneakers. "I'm sorry I was, um, rude before. People are always expecting me to know Spanish because of my looks, and it's super annoying. My Mexican mom left when I was two, but my dad remarried when I was four. *She's* my mom. She treats me and my younger siblings all the same, so people picking on me makes me feel like an outcast in my own family."

"Okay. No biggie. I get it. Thanks for explaining. Sorry about that. Well, my club's all about being outcasts. What's your name so I can stop calling you New Girl in my head?"

"Alicia, but I go by Lease. L-e-e-s-e."

"I'm glad you spelled it for me. I'm Jacinda." We shook hands. "Are you serious about joining my Angels Club? 'Cause we're definitely gonna need more help. Got any talents?"

"Um … nope. I really want to be in it though." Her hesitation made it sound like a lie. Maybe she's shy with hers like I am with singing. "But, I might be able to help you get some money. I have some baseball cards I can sell after school."

"You'd do that?"

"Yep. It's for a good cause. Plus, I got some doubles."

We continued to talk as we went to math class together. She thought horses were okay but was not a big fan. Yeah, I'm going do my best to change that.

After class, I dashed to the office and was out of breath when I got there. "Hi," I said to the secretary. "With 4th/5th grade soccer starting up soon, I was wondering if I could I sell baked goods when the game's on school—"

"Nope," she cut me off. "Can't. Sorry. The student booster club has an exclusive on bake sales."

"Aww, chunky monkey! Kay, never mind then. Wait! Who does the majority of the baking for the student boosters? Kids or the parents?"

"Kids, one in particular does most. Victory Miles. I think you're in the same grade?

Uh, of course *she* does! It just had to be her. And she wins again! I snarled and said, "Icckk. Yeah, I'm certainly familiar. But she's on the competition cheerleading squad. She works with the boosters too?"

"She's enthusiastic and loves to cook, what can I say?"

"Thanks." My balloon of hope popped and it made that farting sound as it sailed and limped to the ground. We really needed someone who could cook. Kat was already getting a list of people in need of favors from her church. There was so much good we could do with yummy treats and food, like providing meals for shut-ins or new moms or people just home from the hospital. But, there was no way on earth I'd ever, ever, ever ask that ME-blaster to join. Not that she would anyway. It was also clear we were gonna have to come up with some way to make money, but, even without the bake-sale roadblock, fundraising probably wouldn't even be allowed here anyway because this wasn't school-affiliated. Lemonade stands were kind of out of season, and there wasn't much traffic down our road anyway. Hmm. I'm sure, with all of us Angels putting our thinking caps on, we can come up with something cool ... and cheap.

I just didn't get that light bulb moment of brilliance yet.

After school, I almost cried when Leese handed me two twenties outside of Angel's barn. Her mom brought her over. "Got a ton of special cards that my dad gave me. The signed Jim Rice baseball card I sold today only graded Excellent Mint, so the most I could squeeze the sports dude for was $40. He tried to low-ball me with $18."

I hugged her. "Oh wow. Oh wow. That's awesome and so sweet of you. Can't believe you did that. Thank you so, so much. We have enough for the mom now, at least to help her out for one week."

"When ya gonna give her the cash? Ya doin' it all together? 'Cause I definitely want to be there."

"Friday after school. She goes there every Tuesday and Friday at 4, so we're gonna leave a gift box with the manager and spy from the pizza shop across the street. Come on. Let me show you around." I didn't start with

Angel, because she wasn't the best representation of a horse right now. So I let her see all of the other horses first, including the borders. When we finally did get to Angel, I held my breath. But Leese, who's not even much of a lover of horses, saw the same inner beauty I had when I first looked into Angel's eyes.

"Well, aren't you a pretty thing?" She stroked Angel's nose.

I hooked the lead line to Angel and led the mare out so Leese could get a better look. Hopefully, she wouldn't gag, seeing her skeletal frame. She didn't. Yay!

"I've never seen a horse like this. She's so adorable."

"Isn't she? She's my very own project horse. I'm gonna turn her out and let her walk around and graze in the back pasture. She just got here Saturday and hasn't been too frolicky the past two days. I'm sure she just needs more nourishment to get her energy back. I noticed she can find the tiniest buds of clover the other horses miss. She's probably used to scrounging for scraps. She didn't get proper food for at least a month, so she has a *long* way to go. I'm supposed to help her get up to a healthy weight and a saleable condition, so she can be sold for money for the therapeutic program."

"Oh no! She's being sold!" Leese cried, reaching out to touch Angels white curls. "That's so sad."

My eyes burned as I said, "Unfortunately, *that's* the plan. But, with any luck, maybe I can change it. I hope. If not … well, I just know I'll spend the rest of my life bawling my eyes out. I've gotta do my best to keep that from happening."

6

On Thursday before going to the farm to work with Angel, I stopped at the library to see if the *Priscilla the Great* book I ordered from another library had come in yet. I locked my bike out front and ran in like Batgirl on a mission. While waiting for the librarian to get off the phone, I played a jazzy drum beat with my fingers on the counter. I really wanted the book, but I was also anxious to zip over to Sunnybrook to see how Angel was doing. Though I *did* have fun with my dad on Tuesday and Wednesday and told him all about my project horse, I hadn't seen my girl since Monday. Maybe she was a little thicker now? A little? I hoped.

I was getting impatient, and my lips ballooned out when I exhaled with a puff, but I coughed in surprise on my very next breath when I heard a familiar voice. A totally gaggifying one. What! I could've sworn I heard Tory's cackle. Was her voice haunting me outside of school now too? What would she be doing in the library? Hmm. Studying how to be *human* would be a nice start.

I cringed as I spun and followed her voice on tiptoe. It sounded like she was reading. I gripped the wooden molding arching over the entrance to the Kid Zone and gasped. She *was* reading. She was sitting on the plush chair with colored circles on it, and kids sat attentive in a half circle around her legs. Holding a picture book out so they could see, she went chirpy as she took on the voice of Mrs. Squirrel. She looked up, and I recoiled and spun past the archway, planting my back against the tan wall. My heart pounded furiously. Her voice carried on with the story. Phew. She didn't see me.

My face must've been too crinkled with confusion because the librarian, now off the phone, waved me over and said, "*Yes*, your book finally came in. Hold on. Let me get it." She quickly found it on the shelf behind her.

"You remember me?"

"You've been badgering me for three weeks. How could I forget?" She tilted her head sideways and gave me a fake mannequin smile.

I pointed to the kid Zone. "Sorry. What's that girl doing in there? Reading to kids?"

"It's the Read-Aloud Program. She does it every Thursday afternoon after school."

Had she actually veered into criminal acts? "Why? Did a judge sentence her to community service or something?"

She glared. "No. She's been doing it over a year now."

"But … why?"

"You know, I know it's hard to believe, but *some*

children," she accentuated, as if *I* were not in that elite club, "actually *like* to reach out and help others."

I looked down, feeling sad. *I'm certainly trying.*

"Since her little sister died, I think doing something nice for children helps Tory feel closer to her."

"Wait! Her sister died? For real?"

"I wouldn't joke about that now." She took my card from me and checked out my book, but I had to curl my lips in to keep a volcanic sob inside.

Tia may be an annoying little gnat at times, but at least she was warm and spinning around like a helicopter and singing way off-key. How horrible! I couldn't imagine losing her!

I grabbed my book and ran out. As soon as my sneakers slapped the gray cement, I bowled over and sobbed my heart and eyes out. Maybe she's really truly mean, some people just are, but maybe, Tory has been mean because it gives her a sense of control or because lashing out comes from a source of pain. Losing a sister must feel like the ground fell out from underneath your feet. I'm gonna smother my impish, jelly-squirting little sister in kisses as soon as I get home and tell her she can be in my club, *if* she can behave. Abuela Rosa's death was hard enough to take. I couldn't imagine life without Tia.

In any case, it was clear Tory *did* have a heart in there somewhere. She also had baking and cooking skills which Angels Club desperately needed. But how on earth could I convince her of that when she won't even talk to me without calling me Taco or Chihuahua? And how could I not gag or cringe at the thought of her being in my room?

Then, she'd be slinging mud as if it's confetti in my own personal horse cave? I won't stand for that. No. No way. There has to be someone else. *Anybody* else. I'd even take the cafeteria lady over that Me-hating Victory Miles.

7

Friday, going to school was entirely different than Monday. The rocks above the door were really confused because I was holding my head and shoulders high today. They scrambled away, totally bummed that there'd be no party. I did a *lot* of thinking about Tory, and I felt like a huge weight was off me because I saw her in a totally different light now. They say knowledge is power. And it is! Once you better understand what you fear, you can face it head-on with confidence. I still didn't want anything to do with her, and inviting her to be an Angel seemed like smashing my own thumb with a hammer, so *that* was never going to happen. But at least I realized she couldn't hurt me anymore. Even though I was the tallest kid in this place, she always made me feel so tiny and pathetic. That was never gonna happen again. You don't always know what's going on in someone's life, and my heart ached for her now. I felt sorry for her, and you can't entirely hate or fear someone you sympathize with. Her tragic, painful circumstances helped me to see that everyone has a story and that I don't always know everything that's hidden in their pages.

But, as much as I wanted to feel like Queen of the Smurfs here, when I saw her in the hallway near my locker talking to Bruce the Brute with Posh beside her, a knot formed in my stomach. I suddenly felt sick, like that time I wasn't paying attention and oopsie-gulped down a spoonful of Lucky Charms in curdled milk. Were they forming a tri-headed beast to attack me now? I could maybe take one at a time, but I wasn't quite ready for multiple chomps. And besides, I had absolutely no sympathy or compassion for Bruce. I could feel my shoulders shrinking. As I got closer, it was clear there was only one head to this beast, and he needed to be sent back to his lair with his tail between his legs.

"Hey, Donkey Butt," Bruce said to Tory with a push on her shoulder. "Not only are you as stubborn as a donkey, you're as ugly as one too, with that high donkey tail." He rocked his torso up and down and heehawed like a donkey.

"It's a ponytail," she muttered, scratching her arms.

"Whatever. It looks ridiculous. The way you twisted it through makes your head look like an ugly donkey's butt."

The hallway was bursting with students, many of them now laughing and pointing at Tory. Okay, I *know* I *should* feel a spark of glee, like boomerang justice had finally gone her way, but seeing her sucker-punched made me feel miserable, especially when I saw the crushed look on her red face and the downturn of her lower lip. I knew she took pride in the way she looked, and he hit her with a very low blow. I actually felt ... *sad* seeing him shred her like that.

Taller than every head here, I could see salt water pooling in Tory's blue eyes. It spilled out unevenly down her cheeks. She bit her pouty lip, surely trying to hold sobs at bay and a sliver of her pride intact. Okay, she may be my worst nightmare and arch nemesis, but he was a vile-mouthed shrimp and he needed to be stopped right now. My tight lips wiggled as I tried to contain my anger, but I was so totally sick and tired of the trash talk in these halls. School should be a safe zone, not a prison where everyone was fighting to be top dog. This was getting so ridiculous! Fuming mad, I booked over there, my long legs moving like super-sonic stilts. The sea of kids parted for me like I'd just smashed down a heavenly staff. "Hey!" I cried.

All giggles stopped abruptly.

As if the flash of silence didn't warn him, Bruce saw me coming right for him and his eyes got wide. He shuffled a couple steps back from me as I met him, elbows-to-face.

"Hey," I repeated, towering over him, glowering. "Why ya talkin' to her like that? The only one lookin' like a donkey here is you because of the way you're acting. She's the prettiest girl in school, besides Posh, and you know it. I see you staring at her all the time, so I *know* you're flat-out lying."

He gawked and turned red that I spilled the beans on his not-so-secret secret.

"But you know what? She'd never ever crush on a boy as rude and obnoxious as you. She's way too smart for that. So give it up." I stared him down, threatening him with my glare alone. "You need to leave people alone. *Every*one. Got it?"

He nodded as he staggered backwards. Then he spun and ran off like a greased piglet being chased.

Tory's wide eyes still ran, and she shook her head, looking stunned. Her rosy lips twitched like she wanted to say something but refused to let the words out.

"Excuse me," I muttered. "I need to get into my locker." I looked over my shoulder. People were watching us, most of them smiling. One girl was even giving me a silent clap, so I believed all the joy spreading around was for my victory over Victory and Bruce at the same time. Even if she hated my guts and wanted to mash 'em with the soles of her baby-blue, glitter sneakers, she'd look like the meanest bully in the world if she insulted me after I stood up for her and rebuilt her rep in the same beautifully brilliant move.

She took her gawking face and bolted away as fast as her legs could move.

In dance class after lunch, even though I was getting better with each week and not so limb-spastic anymore, she kept looking at me with her eyes all weird. Her expression was unreadable. On the way out the door, I must've been staring at her funny too.

She looked around, appearing unnerved. "What are you doing? Is something wrong with your eyes?"

"Nope. You keep looking at me weird."

"I just … I just…" She bit her lip.

"Yes?" I said, drawing out the "e" for emphasis.

"Why'd you, um … stick up for me? After everything I…" She trailed off and crossed her arms with a huff.

"Because *I'm* actually a nice person, and you'd know that if you'd taken the time to find that out instead of using me as your punching bag."

"I never punched you."

"Not with your fists, but plenty with your mouth." I glared at her because I wasn't sure if she was going to give me the true buttered-popcorn jellybean—yum yum, my fave—that I deserved, like, I don't know, a heartfelt apology?

Her clamped lips did that squirm thing again, like she was mad maybe, and she spun away. But she only took two steps and pivoted back. "I'm, uh … sorry," she said so quietly I wasn't sure if she'd actually said it.

"What?" I said, forcing her to repeat it.

She looked over each shoulder. Nope. She was *not* in the clear. We weren't alone, with only Posh at her side this time. People were lingering, paying attention. "I didn't realize how hurtful words can be until today. And I'm sorry for, um, all the mean things I said. I'm sorry. Truly. Okay?"

"I'm wicked sorry too," Posh said. "I had no right to be mean to you."

I was so shocked they actually did it. "Okay. I can't say I'm totally over the stings, but I can move past it and be cool. I forgive you. Kinda." I swirled my hands around. "Are we good here?"

They both nodded.

"Good." I went to walk away but after three steps, I spun and said, "You know? It's too bad you hate me so much, for absolutely no good reason. Because you two are *perfect* for this special thing I have going on. As beautiful and talented as you both are, you could help out so much with..." I stopped myself there, leaving them that dangling carrot. "Ah, forget it. Never mind." I beamed like I was bigger and better than them, well, I *am* bigger, but like I had the world's best-kept secret locked tightly behind my lips. I walked away with a near bounce, knowing their curiosity just got pricked with the sharp pin of my awesomeness.

"Whatcha talkin' about?" Posh cried.

I kept on walking. When I got to the end of the hall, I spun back around. They were still looking my way, their mouths open. I made a C around my lips with my fingers and cried, "Ya know, if you can be nice to me all day and prove your apology and attitude change is legit, then maybe I'll tell you." I flipped them air kisses. "You aren't worthy of knowing such a precious secret if you can't be kind." Twigs to the fire! Yep. I rocked. I went on my merry way with my heart feeling so springy and fresh.

Sure enough, they left me alone, and after school, they caught up with me, their eyes wide with itchiness to know what I refused to tell 'em.

I grabbed Tory's arm, looked over her shoulder and all around. I shushed them with my index finger over my lips for effect. Their noses scrunched in confusion as I waved them to follow me into the bathroom.

"Gonna beat me up?" Tory said.

"No. If I were gonna do that, would'a done it already," I said. When I tacked on the lie, "I know Tae Kwon Do," for good measure, her eyes bugged out.

"You do?" she said, her voice all wavy. "What were you talking about earlier? What special project can I help with?"

"No, not just you. I'm gonna need Posh too. I can't do this without her. She's got fashion sense and knows a ton about helping people look their best. And you can bake like nobody's business."

"Yeah, so?" Posh said with a sneer. "What's that gotta do with anything?"

"Don't know if I should spill it. Not sure you both have what it takes. It might involve some sacrifice. And you two aren't exactly known for being selfless."

Posh said, "As cheer captain of the competition squad, I'm usually so busy choreographing with Coach Tami, but Tory reads for the—" Getting an arm-smack to the stomach and a fiery glare from Tory shut Posh up.

"What's this about?" Tory said, steaming with impatience. "Will you spit it out already?"

"I have a good deeds club. We wanna help everyone from little kids to grannies, but we need more talent in our pool, talent that *you* have."

That shut them up, which I didn't expect. But their eyes were sparkling with the rush of possibilities. Yep. They got the same stirring I did. I could tell before they said yes that they were truly Angels at heart, and my little ragtag team was about to get bigger.

"Oh. And let's get something straight right now. My name's *Jacinda*, not Taco or Burrito Breath." I looked from beautiful girl to beautiful girl. "Well, are you in?"

Posh looked to Tory, and they both did that frowny-faced shrug thing that visually said, "Why not."

"Great. We have seven now. Kat, Emily, Leese, Tia, you two, and myself."

I made up a secret handshake on the fly with my thumb and pinky spread out like spanned wings. After almost busting a gut at the silly dance I made them do as a teensy bit of payback, I said, "Ladies, welcome to Angels Club. We're the Heavenly Seven, and we're going to fill this world with a lot more smiles. You're just in time too. We're giving our first Angels' kiss today."

8

After school, we all, even Tia, slithered into a semi-circle booth by the window in Pop's Pizza. The Heavenly Seven was *on*. We were as giddy and squawky as geese migrating south for winter.

Tory was still giving me crazy eyes, so I think she was still feeling guilty about how she treated me.

The box was safely with the store manager, and we wanted him to give the mom the present on her way out so we could see her reaction. He had no clue what was in it.

Emily had her wheelchair off to the side and was sitting on the end, craning her neck to get around me.

"Wanna switch places?" I asked.

"Nah, I'm better on the end. I can see all right."

I didn't realize the waitress had come up to our table until she cleared her throat to get our attention.

Emily turned her face towards her. "My mom's paying.

She said we could have soda if we wanted, just *one* glass each. So, we'll all take Cokes, one with no ice, and two large pizzas, one meat lovers, one plain cheese. And can I get a side of fries? I like fries with my pizza."

The woman, whose name tag said she was Franny, put her hands on her thighs, bent down to get level with Emily's face and loudly said, "Would you like me to bring you some ketchup?" all blippy and high-pitched like she was talking to a dense one-year-old.

"No, um … just some vinegar please," Emily said, pulling back from her.

"Vinegar?" Franny cried in shock, shaking her tilted head like it had come loose on one side from Emily's very 'incorrect' request. She stood and added, "That's not right, honey."

"Hey!" Kat bellowed. "Don't talk to our friend like that. She's got a whole, functioning brain, just like anybody else. She doesn't need baby talk, shouting like she's deaf, or people all up in her face. It's very patronizing and rude. And she wants vinegar, *not* ketchup, so give her vinegar."

That made Emily smile bigger than I'd ever seen. Maybe that was the first time she actually felt like she had real friends.

Tory and Posh were very quiet and looked so unmistakably guilt-ridden.

"Sorry," the red-faced waitress said. At least she reset her head to straight. "Never had anyone request vinegar before."

"It's a Canadian thing," Emily said. "My dad's from Quebec. Got any?"

"Hmm. I'll check. Again, I apologize for that. I'll be right back with your drinks."

Emily looked to the side and batted my arm. "Hey. Look! Look! The wagon! That's her. There she is."

She had her baby in a Radio Flyer wagon, which she left outside. She slid her tot into a cart seat and the automatic doors opened for her like she was a queen when she rolled across the sensor.

"Wow. You weren't kidding about young," Leese said. "And she's tiny too."

"I know. She gets like two to three bags of groceries at a time and some milk usually."

We were soon busy, sipping our drinks, chowing down pizza, and trying to figure out our next Angels' kiss.

Tia had her back to the window more than anyone. But after several minutes of squirming around, she got tired of not being able to see and got up on her knees and peered out with her hands on the back of the leather seat.

"Sit down, Tia. She'll probably be in there another ten minutes."

"I can't see. It's not fair. I got the worst seat."

Tory, to my surprise, squealed the loudest and covered her mouth and nose with her joined fingers when the mother finally came out with her bags.

"See? *Mira mira*," Tia shrilled with a finger point, telling me to look. "Told you. I would'a missed it."

The teen looked all around as if searching for hidden cameras. She squinted at the little blue box like it might contain an alien creature. When she untied the white ribbon and opened it, she slapped her lips.

We'd exchanged our fistfuls of cash with the biggest bills we could, and she took it out and counted it. Even though I couldn't see her tears, I could tell she was crying. She crouched down and looked up to heaven, as if thanking God for this unexpected blessing. Her hand looked to be shaking as she pulled out our calling card and read it.

"She found the note too," Posh said. "I so love that idea. It's the cutest thing ever."

"Oh my gosh, look how happy she is," Emily said while clapping. "She has tears of joy. I knew it!"

The mother stood and started spinning. She picked up her baby and gave him at least a dozen kisses.

"Awww, that's so sweet and precious, I could cry," Kat said.

"What! You? Cry? Don't tell me you're turning all mushy on me," I teased her.

"Well, maybe. A *little*. She's worth the softer heart."

"What's it say? What's it say?" Tia said, spinning with a flop down onto her butt.

"'*Angels smiled on you today. Go be an angel too*'," I said.

"Cool. I really like that," Tory said, snatching some of Emily's fries from the middle of the table.

I hugged Em. "Me too. I feel all cozy inside. Don't you?"

She nodded. *Tory* nodded. My worst nightmare nodded. Maybe we could end up friends.

"This was the perfect first kiss, Em," I said. "And with more money from Tory and Posh pooled in, I'm sure we made her week."

We cheered in celebration and our clamor grew as a million angelic ideas bubbled up in my mind.

"Soooo," Kat said, "who we gonna *kiss* next?"

"I don't know," I said and shrugged, looking up from my pad. "We got a whole world of possible targets. Good thing there are seven of us."

9

Not only was I jumping around like a bean because Angels Club was on a roll and school would be worlds better now with Bruce and Tory off my back, but my lovely Angel was starting to look a lot more heavenly. I kinda figured she'd look like a unicorn in her true glory. And she so totally does! I was chomping at the bit—all horse intended—to groom Angel and clean her ears some more, so I zipped over to Sunnybrook right after breakfast. Therapy doesn't start until noon, giving me plenty of time to spend with her. Since Sunday, I'd given her another sudsy bath, and she looked stunning now. *I* swear she's gaining weight too, although Mrs. M says it's too soon for there to be any real difference.

She's fluffy and sparkling white, and her mane hangs in shiny ringlets. Her long wavy tail and her fetlocks are spotless. She doesn't even roll in the dirt right now like the other horses. I think she's sick of dirt at the moment.

The farrier came and trimmed her hooves, but he said they were strong and hard, and with another couple of trims, she should be perfect. That pleased Mrs. M, who thought the lack of care might've harmed her in some way. A horse that doesn't get their hooves trimmed every six weeks or so can have too much growth and develop problems, but Angel was fine.

"Hi, Angel. How ya doin'?" I called out, entering the barn. I hustled to the tack room to fetch my grooming box. I have my own purple box with my name on the side. My dad surprised me with it when he learned I was volunteering here. I love it so much and make sure my brushes stay clean and organized. It holds a curry brush, a stiff-bristled brush, two soft body brushes—one that Ginger especially loves, a comb for the mane and tail, and a horse pick to clean hooves. Today, I added a soft cloth and a bottle of water to wash Angel's ears. I put my special box on the floor next to the crossties so it was ready to use, and then went to Angel's stall to get her.

"Angel," I called and gave a short whistle. Her head was already out of the stall. She neighed softly to say 'hello', and I dug into my jean pocket for a horse cookie. "Got a treat for you," I sang.

Her soft eyes twinkled like stars as I approached. Her curly mane gleamed now, and her once-tangled and mud-caked forelock was soft and white. The corkscrew waves between her eyes went down to the tip of her nose.

I opened my fingers and held my hand flat. She picked the cookie up with soft lips, and I stroked her head and scratched between her ears. "There ya go, pretty girl.

Ready to get brushed?" I reached for her halter, and she kept her head over the stall door so I could put it on. I clipped on the lead line, opened the stall, and walked her to the crossties. "Good girl."

She was one smart horse, my Angel girl! I know the McKinleys wanna sell her, but if I can't come up with a way to get her to stay, my heart'll just ... explode. I've only known this white princess a week, and the thought of losing her to another forever home was like getting tiger claws to the chest. I blinked away tears and cleared my throat. "There you go, girl. Today we'll tackle those ears. They're definitely cleaner than when you first got here, but I wanna see if I can get more dirt out and the blood crusties." The curls and hair kept a lot of dirt out, but I could see specks beyond the wispy curtains. I led Angel and clipped her to the crossties for grooming. As soon as the clip clicked, she whinnied and scraped her hoof on the floor.

Sure enough, I heard Emily's wheelchair as she entered the barn. This horse feels a special bond with her. She knew she was coming and greeted her with joy. I spun and smiled. "Hi, Em"

Emily wheeled up to Angel and me and stopped. "Hi, Jacinda. I came a little early to help. Is that okay?" she said with her usual wide smile.

"Yeah, definitely. Did ya hear that? When you were coming up? Her whinny and hoof scrape? She's so thrilled to see *you* specifically. So awesome!"

"Really?" she sang with a huge smile that turned into a gawk. "Wow. That's so cool."

"Yep. You're special to her. She can see how amazing you are."

"She probably doesn't care that I walk funny or roll around then."

"Nope. Not one bit."

"I love you soooo much, Angel. I bet you're the nicest horse on the planet. You really are an angel. It's your perfect name. I brought you a treat. Look." She held her hand out flat like I taught her and Angel gently took the peppermint she offered. "Kat may have banned you from mints, but not me. Hee hee. A horse as sweet as you should get sweet treats once in a while." She ran her fingers through her shiny curls. "Oh my goodness. She looks fantastic now, so pretty. You were right! Just like a unicorn. She looks like the one your Abuela Rosa gave you. Can I brush her sides?"

"She'd love that. Let me get you a brush. Careful not to run over my grooming box." I took a brush out and handed it to Emily. "Start here." I pointed to the side that would be easiest for her to reach. I needed to use the curry brush first, but I wanted to give her something to do.

"I can stand up and lean on Angel for support," she insisted.

"You sure?"

"Yes! I can do *some* things by myself you know." Emily was getting stressed out. I knew she wanted out of the wheelchair as much as possible. "I'm getting a lot better on crutches and standing against stuff. I only use the chair out of the house. Watch out, Boston runners, here I come."

I laughed. "*I'd* sure get out of your way. What time's your lesson? I haven't checked the list yet."

"One."

"Good. You've got time."

"What's that for?" she asked, pointing to the brush in my hand.

"It's a curry brush. The soft rubber bristles loosen dirt under a horse's coat. You just keep brushing and I'll use the curry." It would be too much for her to hold her balance and use the curry, and she was just as happy using the soft brush anyway.

I began on the opposite side from Emily and began making short circular movements. Her body was still skinny, and I was very gentle. She didn't have enough fat to take too much pressure. Angel let out a huge sigh and blew through her nose.

"Ugh! She almost hit my nose with stuff!" Emily laughed. "I can tell she loves to be brushed."

"She sure does. And you're doing great. You love this, don't you, Angel?" I finished currying her side and asked Em to switch to get the dirt that was sitting on top of her coat. When we changed places, I used my stiff brush and gently brushed it away. Next, I picked up my extra soft brush and swept it down her legs and fetlocks. Her clean, white fetlocks swirled as I brushed. I knew it was harder to keep a white horse clean, but Angel was worth every minute. She stood quietly, and I could tell she was enjoying the attention from Em and me.

"I looked up American Curly horses after you said that's what she might be," Em said as she leaned against Angel with the brush. "I think you're right. She looks so much like the pics I saw." Angel didn't move an inch. I knew she could feel Em leaning on her for balance. This horse was something else. Em sat back down in her chair. I was proud of her. She was getting braver and braver, and I couldn't wait to see her on Ginger at today's lesson.

"What'd you learn?" I asked as I wet the cloth to clean Angel's ears.

"Well, they're kinda rare. In the winter, they have all types of curls, and the manes and forelocks are wavy, just like Angel's. Also, look at Angel's swirly eyelashes. That's a Curly trait. They shed their coats in spring, which can be spun like wool, but they usually keep their curly tails and manes. And did you know they were considered sacred by the Native American Indians?"

"Yep. Kat sent me some info and I read it all. Angel's a very special horse." I pressed my wet cloth into Angel's ears. They were finally healing. At first, she didn't like it and tossed her head. I knew they were sore. The salve Mrs. M gave me had done a good job. I kept at it and got the soft cloth further in and she stood quietly for the first time. Emily was jabbering about something or other, but I was concentrating on cleaning Angel's ears better so I could put on more salve. I'd never seen a horse with curls in and around the ears.

"Are her ears clean now? I read Curly horses have those curls to protect their ears from bugs." Em was watching me intently.

"Some bugs did get in, but lucky for Angel, she had the guard of curls 'cause her ears would've been even worse."

The soft cloth was stained with dry blood. I was surprised she let me do as much as I did. I took another look inside her right ear and saw a blue mark. "What the ... what on earth is that?"

"What?" Em asked looking up at the ear.

"I don't ... know. Some blue mark, but it's hidden by her hair. Hold on." I stood on my toes to look closer. "Think it might be some kinda design, but it's hard to see."

"Is it a tattoo?" Emily was very interested and excited. "I read where some horses get tattooed so an owner can identify their horses."

"Maybe it is."

She crooned her neck like a crane. "I wanna see! Here, take a pic with my phone so we both can get a better look." Emily handed me her phone.

I held it close to Angel's ear, and *click*... there it was. To be sure I had a clear one, I took two more before handing the phone back.

"Wow. Cool. I can knock it out in Photoshop and hunt this down with an image search."

"That'd be awesome! I'd love to know where she came from."

Using her fingers, she nimbly swept the touch pad out to enlarge the picture of Angel's ear so we could get a better look.

"Huh, that's weird," I said.

We both stared at the picture of a circle with the letters CKT and what looked like a tiny crown above the letters.

"Looks like a logo maybe," Emily said. "But you're the horse expert. Mean anything to you?"

"*Nada*," I muttered, with my brain in a cloud. "I mean, *nope*, nothing."

"Well, maybe some research'll tell us."

"That'd be great. 'Cause I don't have any clue." Hopefully, Emily would be able to figure out where Angel came from and where she got that mysterious tattoo. I was so itching to know.

"Mami!" I cried, walking into our kitchen, as soon as I got back home. "Need help with dinner?"

"*Gracias mija,*" she said, thanking me with the cutesy abbreviation for 'my daughter'. "But I'm just making spaghetti. Water's boiling now. You can cut the Italian bread though."

"Kay. Cool." I washed my hands and got a knife out of the drawer.

She was watching me.

"What."

"*Nada.* I just like that you're a lot more helpful these days, not just with me, but *everyone.*"

I grabbed the paper bag with the bread and the wooden board. "Well, I'm trying. I'm even reaching out to try to make some new friends at school."

"That's wonderful. So, does that mean you can let me know about your party? I'll need a head count."

"Why a head count? Please tell me you're not doing anything major. I told you I didn't want you to throw a big party for me. You can't afford it. A cake and a couple people over is all I need." I sliced the bread and picked up the heel to munch because no one but me eats those.

"I have a special surprise. And don't worry about the cost. You've earned this party with all the good work you've been doing."

"Okay. If you're sure. I don't know who I want to invite though. I'm still thinking about it. I have an idea, but not sure all of them'll come."

"Well, I'll need to know by Monday. It's this Friday night."

"All right. I'll let you know. I definitely want Kat to come, and Emily. She did so awesome at therapy today. Oh my goodness, you should've seen her. She was able to hold her balance, and she let go of the horn, so Miss Jane let her circle the ring twice without a side walker. She rocked it. Her smile glowed like the moon."

"She's such a sweet girl. I'm glad she found the courage to ride. I'm sure it'll help her, as you've seen the benefit with other kids."

"It will. I know it." I started slicing the bread again. "Oh! Kat asked me over her house for dinner tomorrow night, but I blurted out a 'yes' before I asked permission. Can Tia and I go?"

"What?" She gawked with a suspicious smile. "You want Tia to go? Did I miss something or did one of the horses kick you in the head? You're not playing a joke on *her* this time, are you?"

I laughed and brushed cornmeal off my hands. "Nooo. She just promised she'd try to be less annoying. If she can be cool, then I don't mind her tagging along from time to time." I put all the slices in a basket and covered it with an unfolded napkin. "So, can we go? Please?" I threaded my fingers together to beg.

"Sure. But I don't want you out too late. I'll pick you up at eight."

I jumped up and down. "*Gracias.*" Awesome. Now everyone in Angels Club could brainstorm and nail down the targets for our Angels' kisses for the next couple of weeks!

Between all the ideas running through my head and the mystery of Angel's tattoo, I had a hard time concentrating on my vocab words, so I put them to song to help me remember the definitions. If only coming up with lyrics were that easy, then I'd write music for babies in the hospital. That'd be amazing. So glad Emily brought it up. When I saw her number on my phone, I screeched. "Hi, hi! Find anything out about the tattoo?"

"Yes, yes, yes," she twittered. "And you're not gonna believe it. Angel used to be a *circus* horse! I even found a pic of her on the site that confirms it. So incredible. The letters CKT belong to a small, traveling circus. CKT stands for Charles King Topper, and I guess the crown's used because of his middle name."

"Oh, wow, oh wow. That's the coolest thing ever."

"I know. I almost burst when I saw that. I read more and watched vids about circus horses and they can do the coolest things. Think she knows any tricks?"

The buzz of excitement in my brain was like a hundred bees had just made a home of it. "I don't know! What cool things can they do? Like what?"

"Well, I saw clowns and acrobats doing handstands and scary holds and body twists on their backs. And as horses circle the arena at a trot, a rider jumps on or off, while the horse just keeps going. At the end of its time in the ring, it can bow to the audience. And the most amazing thing I saw was a horse laying down at some kind of command so a shorter rider, or a girl like me in a chair, could get on and then it, ta-da, stands up. Can you imagine how cool it would be if Angel knew how to do that? Kids like me wouldn't even need mounting blocks."

I screamed and started jumping up and down and dancing with a crazy twirl. "Oh my gosh, Emily! This is it! If Angel can really do those things, especially lay down to let a rider on, then Mrs. M would have to let her stay! She'd have to! None of the horses at Sunnybrook can do that. I just need to find the cues she may have been taught in the circus. Can you look up more videos? I'll do the same, but you may be able to find some better ones than me that show the cues clearly."

"Sure! I'll look around. Another cool thing is, you know how Angel didn't even spook when that big hay truck drove up today? She didn't even budge! Well, circus horses *have* to be calm with noises, either from loud music or people screaming, clapping or whistling.

"That's another added benefit too. Emily! Oh my goodness. I just got the best idea ever. What if you rode her in the fundraiser showcase and we showed everyone how great she is? We can work together to get both you and her ready and surprise everyone. We can make people think you're going to ride Ginger, but we'll switch and you'll really ride Angel instead. I just know she's amazing, like, the best horse for therapy, ever. And I'm going to prove it."

"My parents have signed me up for twice a week now because I love it so much, but do you think I'll be ready for the showcase? Or that she will be? You said you haven't even ridden her yet. What if she can't be ridden? And isn't that only like three weeks away?"

"I'm not worried about the time. She'll be a bit too thin still, but you have a point about the riding. I guess we'll just have to let Angel show us what she's capable of. For the first time since meeting her, I have hope now, real hope, that maybe, just maybe, she'll have a way to stay, and I'll be able to convince Mrs. M that she totally belongs here. Thank you, Charles King Topper! Got any contact info for the circus?"

"Hold on."

I waited a minute, and Emily rattled off a phone number for me. I scratched it down with my purple feather pen and looked at it with a smile. "If Angel can do all these things while being as sweet as sugar pie, then I wonder how she ended up with the old man."

"I don't know. Maybe the circus'll be able to tell you."

"Oh my word! I'm so excited, Emily. This could be the answer to everything. We have to do whatever we can to try to get Mrs. M to change her mind. Angel's our friend. I refuse to let her go. Not without a really good fight."

10

"Meeting's in session," Tory said as we were clustered around the round picnic table on Kat's flagstone patio. "Come to order."

I scoffed. "What are you doing? This isn't *Judge Judy*."

"Yeah," Tia said with a sneer. "You sound like a batman, some wannabe cop."

"That's a *bailiff*," I corrected her. "Not a batman. And I'm pretty sure bailiffs are real cops and that *judges* call a court to order. I think. But we don't have to be so formal, Tory. Let's just, I don't know … *talk*."

Tory stood up to pace and waved her hands. "No, we *need* a leader, or else there'll be chaos, especially when it's a bunch of girls involved. I've been in *plenty* of clubs. Trust me. I know."

"Well, I don't have a problem with anyone." I looked at Posh because she was surely the only one here who might. "Do you?"

ANGELS CLUB

She shrugged. "Nah, don't look at me, girl. I'm cool."

"Okay then. Look," I said, "this club was my idea, and *I* say we keep things loose. If anyone, *I* should be the leader, but I want *everyone* to have equal say. Everyone gets to contribute to our list of kisses for the next week or so. At the pizza shop on Friday, we all were given the task of thinking of things to do and how we can use our talents to help others. We can list all our ideas and figure out what to do first. We can't do everything in one week though, so we'll roll things out and do what we can as we can. All of us have limited time, and Tia can't bike anywhere alone. Plus, she's still on training wheels…"

"Hey!" She whacked my arm with the back of her hand. "You didn't have to rat me out! You're making me sound like a baby."

"Well, it's *true*. And you do babyish stuff all on your own. You don't need my help to expose you. But maybe we can teach you how to ride. How's that?"

She nodded with squinty eyes like she was suspicious. "Better."

"Good. Okay. So, we'll have to just … um, do things here and there. And we'll start with Kat's ideas. What'd you come up with?"

"Well, I definitely wanna draw pictures for the military. Emily found this cool website for me called Any Soldier, and servicemen and women list exactly what they want and need. Maybe we can send a care package too."

"Great! We can probably send some drawings, but we can't afford to send a care package right now. With the new money from Posh and Tory, we have twenty-three dollars in our pot, so some to work with, but not a lot. We can maybe send a package if we come up with a way to raise more money. That'd be really nice for Thanksgiving or Christmas. We can't have Leese selling off any more baseball cards. That's not fair to ask."

"What about my idea for horse pictures," Tia said, "to sell at the show?"

"No one's gonna buy your dumb horse pictures."

Tia growled at me and clenched her fists. "You *said* to think of what we're good at, and I'm good at crafts. I have tons of paper and white cardstock, so it'll be free. I've seen this paper horse online with swivel legs that we can make. Kat can draw the outlines, and we can cut them out and decorate them. We can put the cut-out horses on heavy, colored paper and frame them with white cardstock. Maybe we can do different breeds."

"You know, it's not a bad idea," Kat said, patting Tia's little head. "It might be cute. I haven't seen anything like that at a show. Have you?"

"No," I groaned. "Probably because no one would buy such a thing."

Kat shrugged. "Maybe no one's thought of it yet. We can at least *try* it and make fifteen or so. I like it."

Tia was pouting that I disregarded her idea, but she beamed and looked at me smugly like the best idea creator in the universe when Kat backed her up.

"Okay, okay," I gave in, waving my hands in surrender. "It's a good idea, Tia. Kinda. But I don't think we'll get much money with that alone. Even if we sold them for five dollars each, I can't imagine that being a big seller. I do like the idea of selling at the fundraiser, but we need something really cool to sell too. Let's get back to Kat. What else did you wanna do?"

"That care package idea was all I had, but Tia's idea gave me a new one. In addition to the get-well letters, we could create fall decorations for the children's hospital."

"I'm not goin' into any hospital," Tory cried, shaking her head. "Uh uh. No way."

"Don't worry. Your precious, wavy hair won't have to soak up the smell of Lysol," Kat blurted out. "We can—"

"Kat!" I cried, cutting her off with chastisement. She had no clue about Tory's dead sister. "Be nice." My heart hurt for Tory now. Her eyes were all wet, like she just got punched.

"I'm just saying, we can drop off a box. Or have it delivered. We won't have to go in necessarily."

"Yes! That's a great idea," Leese said. "There's also a women and children's shelter by my house, so maybe we can double up and send some over that way too, just to spread some autumn cheer. I know one of the mentors who works there."

"Really?" Posh asked. "Hmm. Think we could plan a dance party for the kids or something like that? They gotta be bored outta their skulls. *I* sure would be. Tory and I can make snacks and get our hands on some costume pieces and cool music. It doesn't have to be Halloween-themed, just a fall party with some accessories. I can help the girls look all fancy. My cousin's a manicurist, and I've learned all about nail art from her. I can do maybe fifty different designs."

"Cool," I said. "That's fabulous! I love it. Maybe we can do that in a couple weeks. Check with the mentor you know, Leese. See, everyone? This is what we need. The more heads we have to brainstorm, the easier it'll be to bounce and build off each others' ideas." I jotted down those plans and sipped tart lemonade through my straw. "Ahhh. How 'bout you, Leese? Whatcha got?"

She shrugged and hugged herself. "I dunno. I'm not really good at anything." I could tell she was holding back and not wanting to admit her talent. "I can throw a mean curveball and know a ton of fun facts about sci-fi, but those aren't really gonna help here."

"Hey, I love sci-fi too," cried Emily. "I watch anything that has to do with space or aliens or robots."

"Wow. Cool. We'll have to talk about our favorite shows later. It's so hard to meet other fun, quirky geeks." Leese smiled and muttered, "I *am* kind of good at something, Jacinda, I just don't know if I want to like, share it. I'm not sure it'll help anyway."

"Well, what is it? You can tell us."

"Man, it's so lame," she said with a severe cringe. She blocked her eyes for a moment with her fingers. "Uh, it's bad, it's bad."

"Nothing's lame here."

"I can, uh, kinda write a little bit … like prose."

"Prose. I don't know what that is."

"Like poems or even stories in free verse."

"Ha ha!" Tory cried. "That *is* lame."

"No it's not! Be quiet!" I shouted and got up to my feet. She cowered and her lips curled in. "Everyone's talent can help, so don't tease her. This is exactly why she didn't want to share it, because of people like you who will laugh at her. It's *not* lame. It's brilliant. And it just so happens I need someone with exactly that talent. What about songwriting, Leese? Think some of your poems could be added to melodies? Because I play guitar and sing a *little* and want to write lullabies or soft songs for babies, or whoever really, but I need a lot of help coming up with the words."

Her eyes lit up. "Yeah, maybe some of them! I'd love that."

"Me too," I said.

"See?" Emily said. "We all work better as a *team* than apart. We need each other. Let's not fight or be mean. I'm so tired of mean people. We need to be different than other people if we want to spread smiles around."

"I agree," I said, taking my seat again. "How 'bout you, Tory? Come up with anything?"

"Yes, as a matter of fact." She sat down, joining the rest of us. "I was thinking, we could sell baked goods at the farm fundraiser too. *And* I was also thinking about what Kat said before we left the restaurant about the shut-ins and moms at her church. If you can get a short list for me and learn what people need, then I can get some meals over throughout the week."

"Cool," Kat said. "Consider it done."

"There'll be other food vendors at the event though," I said, "but if we have something unique, it might work. I don't know though. I still think we need something cool and different. Emily? How 'bout you?"

"You didn't ask me!" Tia cried.

"Be patient, Teacup. And didn't you already go kinda? You mentioned the horse cutouts."

"Well, I have more to say. It's really, *really* important." She squirmed like she had to pee.

"In a minute. You're next. Em?"

She flipped her red curls over her shoulders. "Um, well I spoke with the senior center, and I'm gonna start giving surfing lessons next week."

"What! You surf?" Posh cried, astonished.

Emily, Kat and I cracked up.

"I wish," Emily said when she caught her breath. "I *meant* on the internet. And I'll also get the names of people who need help with cleaning and leaf raking. Even in a chair, I'm capable of raking or cleaning lower surfaces. I can sit on stairs and use a little hand broom and dustpan, vacuum carpets, clean toilets and bathroom sinks or whatever. I've been doing those things anyway at home for therapeutic purposes, and I'm getting really good at it."

"Wow. That's great, Em. Good thinking." I wrote her ideas down. "Kat's dad might let us use some rakes."

"Me now? Me now?" Tia clapped.

"Yes, Tia." I said, followed by a big sigh. "Uuhhh, it's your turn. *Go.* What's your fabulous idea?"

"You should sing at the show." She giggled and slapped her mouth with both hands.

"Nooo. This was supposed to be how *you* can help. Your idea. How would *me* singing at the show help anyone? I don't get it."

"Yeah, Jacinda," Emily said. "You got on my case for being afraid to ride a horse, but yet, you won't do the thing you're afraid of? You really should sing."

Of course she'd bring that up and chuck it in my face. "No way. Again, I will stress that there's no point."

"If you make a song by then, with Leese helping," Tia said, "you could sing with your guitar and sell CDs."

"Nah. No way. We don't even have a studio to record in, so it'll sound awful."

"We may not have a studio," Posh said, "but Tory and I have done recordings just for fun at the booth at Mick's Bowl. You can shoot video too on the blue screen if you want. Comes out pretty good."

"Yeah, that'll sound so sweet with crashing pins in the background," I spat.

Posh laughed and said, "No, silly. We can go in just before it opens and record a couple takes. And my brother does beats, so he can add some musical riffs and percussion if needed, and mix it all with Pro Tools."

I shook my head and hands. "I have no clue what Pro Tools is."

"It's a program that helps record, mix and smooth out music. Ever hear early stuff by The Black Keys? It's pretty muddy and *that's* a professional band. We can get it good enough to sell at the show, and it probably would sell if you wrote about horses or the inspiration they bring."

"Ugh, errr." She had a point. An ugly, icky, painfully good one. I cringed and felt like I was melting into a puddle and kinda wished I would. I'd rather eat worms than sing in front of people. "I don't know who

The Black Keys are, but okay. If you say so. Maybe. I'll *think* about performing."

Tia clapped, and so did Emily. "Yay!" Tia said. "It'll be so cool. Do it! Do it!"

"So you can pick on me forever? Yeah, not cool," I mumbled and rolled my eyes. "But whatever."

"What's *your* idea," Tia asked. "Tell us, tell us!"

"Well, I do like these mostly out-in-the-open things everyone has come up with, but I was thinking it'd be cool to do more things in secret. Emily, Kat and I kind of floated the idea around initially, but I really like it. I like the point of the Angel's Club being about the people we help rather than us, that we do things just to make someone's day brighter and not necessarily because we wanna be famous or get badges or city ribbons in return. And that could be as simple as leaving a note on someone's car in a store parking lot or a bigger tip or a good luck charm for a waitress when we're in a restaurant with our parents, any little thing that'll make a difference."

"What's considered a good luck charm?" Leese asked.

"Oh, there's all kinds. Four-leaf clovers, random pennies you spot, horseshoes, wishbones, rainbows."

"Too bad we can't bottle a rainbow," Posh said. "Beauty *always* sells. I didn't know they were good luck too." She glanced over her shoulder towards the barn and then back at Kat. "Hmm. Got any horseshoes lying around?"

"Oh, yeah," Kat said. "Are you kidding me? There are boxes of 'em everywhere. My dad just saves 'em for whatever lame reason."

Posh gasped and her pearly white smile gleamed as it got wider. "Think he'd give us some, to, like, sell?"

Kat sneered and said, "Yeah ... I guess. But who'd want a dumb old horseshoe. They're a dime-a-dozen for the folks who come here."

"But, not with my designs on 'em. Remember how I said I can paint nails? Well, I can put those designs on just about anything, *including* horseshoes. We can spray paint 'em as a base, and then cover them with beads, buttons, ribbons, or my painted flowers, swirls, tiger stripes, butterflies or anything else that seems cool."

"Oh my goodness! Posh!" I cried. "That's so amazing and perfect. That's it. You just found our key seller. With all our cool and varied things to sell, we'll have the coolest tent ever! It'll represent all of us and the things we do. I love it."

Everyone nodded in agreement.

"We should also have a Need Box," Emily suggested. "People often have needs you can't see or don't care to notice, and we might be able to find some new targets to kiss through that."

"Love it," I said.

"So, what secretive thing were you thinking of doing first?" Kat asked.

"We should do something nice for your mom, actually," I said, taking my voice down to a whisper. "She's so sweet and does so many things to help others. We should make a big banner and get all the kids to stick their painted hand prints on it and sign it, and then hang it up at the fundraiser to show everyone how much we love and appreciate her. What do ya think? I just don't want her to know *we* did it."

"She'll probably figure it out it was us," Kat said. "She's super smart. But I'm sure she'll love it and probably cry. You know how she is."

"I know. We all set then?"

We all put our hands together and closed our meeting with the shout, "Angels Club, woo!"

After celebrating our ideas and stuffing our faces, Kat and I, oh, and Emily too, proudly showed the girls all the horses at Sunnybrook, even my precious, lovely Angel.

Emily was excited to tell them everything she'd learned about American Curly horses and the unique qualities of the breed.

I think they all loved Angel immediately. She just has those kind of eyes that suck you in and say, "Love me." How could anyone not? She was the best horse in the whole wide world.

11

My insides were buzzing and twinkling like a sparkler when I woke up the next day. I really don't think Mondays are gonna be as nightmarish as they have been, from here on out. Tory and Posh were definitely being a *lot* nicer, and Bruce the Brute was terrified of me now. Every time he spotted me in the hall last Friday, he'd turn and bolt the other way. I really didn't mean to scare him into practically peeing in his pants, but oh well, at least he was out of not only my hair but everyone else's. I hoped people didn't see *me* as the bully now. That was down-right laughable.

I sniffed. Aahhh. I could smell the eggs and bacon cooking, as well as blueberry coffee. I wasn't allowed to have coffee, but I sure liked the way it smelled, especially any fruity or chocolaty ones.

"Mami!" I cried, walking into the kitchen. "Thanks for making me breakfast and for making the eggs cheesy like I love. I know who I wanna invite now, but I need all the deets."

"The deets?" She laughed. "What's that?"

"You know, where and what time. You said Friday, right?"

"Oh yeah. Yes, it's gonna be Friday, five o'clock at the McKinley's. Your father'll be there too. Got the night off."

I crinkled my nose. "At the McKinley's?" I went to ask why, but then said, "Well, yeah, they do have a bigger house. Mrs. M doesn't mind?"

"Nope. Not at all. Don't you think it's a wonderful place to have your party, right in the middle of the things you love most?

"I love my family most. But horses are a close second." I winked at her. "Thank you for my surprise, Mami. That was so sweet of you."

"I'll bring a pizza, or two, depending on how many can come, some drinks and a cake."

I kissed her cheek. "Thank you, Mami. Love you so much. I'm excited for it *now*. It *is* the most perfect spot."

I went to school feeling a lot lighter, and no rocks jumped on me again today to weigh me down. No bullies either, not even Misty. I think they're through with me, thank goodness. But the day kind of sludged along because all I could think about was contacting the circus and learning more about Angel. I fired off an email Saturday night but hadn't heard back, so I was aching to call and talk to a live person. And I was also hoping to ride Angel. I was already planning this whole Emily thing with great excitement to keep Angel here, but what if she couldn't even be ridden? I called Kat and told her all about my plan with Emily, and she thought it was a great idea. I certainly hope so.

I rode my bike to the McKinley's as fast as I could and sped up to Angel's barn. After grooming her and giving her an apple, I loosely set the thickest saddle pad in the barn on the center of her back and one of the smaller amber leather saddles over that. I kept telling her how pretty she looked. She didn't step back or give me any hassles.

I couldn't tell if she was being so calm because she's just so good or because she was too zapped of energy to care. I patted her rump so she'd know I was walking behind her to check the other side. "Such a good girl."

She whinnied and scraped her foot when she saw me get the bridle. I took that as definite, "Yes, about time." She wasn't just being docile, she actually *wanted* to be ridden. By me! At that realization, freshly baked strawberry cupcakes filled my heart and I swear I could smell the yummy-sweet scent. "Look at you. You're so excited, Angel. Makes two of us."

I rubbed her between the ears and she lowered her head so I could slip the bridle on. I placed a thumb into the back of her mouth and she opened it to take the bit. Since she clearly hasn't been ridden in a long while, I expected a head shake, even though she basically gave me an open-invite. I eased the crown over her ears and fluffed her forelock curls down. "Oh my goodness, you look so beautiful all dressed up. You didn't fight or fuss at all. Not sure if I'm gonna ride you *today*, even though I know you

want the attention. I just want to see if you can be decked
out." I walked around her, checking out the saddle on
both sides.

She was still okay wearing the saddle loose, so while
facing forward, I reached under her belly to get the cinch.
I slowly tightened it with several passes through the
saddle ring until it was snug. I tied a cinch knot and
buckled the strap.

I stepped in front of her so I could talk to her and give
her some time to get used to the tighter saddle. "Your
friend, Emily, wants to show you off at the showcase. I do
too, so we have a *lot* of work to do to get you ready. I want
everyone to see how amazing you are, especially Mrs. M.
My heart'll be crushed into dust if someone buys you and
takes you away from me. I sure want you to stay here too,
and I'll do my best to make that happen. But you need to
do your part too, okay?" Tears fell because the pain of
losing her was unimaginable. I clutched Angel's face
gently and kissed her on the nose. She let out a soft nicker.

I gathered the reins and led her out of the barn. She
didn't give me any trouble and walked easily behind me as
I brought her to the round pen. I bit my lip and looked
over my shoulder, weirdly feeling like I was doing
something bad for just having the strong desire to ride her.
But I couldn't help it. She was acting like a princess and
she looked like a unicorn. "You're so skinny, Angel, I
really don't think I should sit on you quite yet, even
though I really, really, really want to. Maybe Friday I'll
saddle you up again before my party and try riding you
then, okay? That'll give you another five days of good food

to give you more energy and stamina. Love you so much." I kissed her nose again.

After a half hour of working with her, I brought her back to the barn. She was *perfect* for me. I cried the entire time I took her riding gear off and put everything in its proper place. Separation from her was blistering because I knew every day she got healthier and stronger, the closer she got to sale. I couldn't let that happen.

When I got home, I called the circus twice and got no answer. I'd invited all the Angels to my party when I was at school, and they all called to say they were coming, so I let my mom know.

The third time I called the CKT Circus, I'm not sure if it was because of all the pretty-pleases I was praying with my fingers clasped together so tight or if it was just my lucky day, but someone, finally, finally picked up. Yes! But they referred me to Lloyd, an animal handler, so I had to wait. And wait. I clocked my tongue in my mouth.

"Yell-oo," a guy said.

I scrunched my face. "Hi, um, are you Lloyd?"

"Still and always."

"Uh, good. I have a horse that used to belong to your circus. I found your tattoo in her ear, and I wanted to find out more information about her. Who would I speak to?"

He huffed in very apparent impatience. "Jed Janik's the horse handler. How long ago was it?"

"Uh, *maybe* two years ago. A picture of this particular horse is on your website. She's on page six of the gallery. I taped her and she's a 14.2-hand, white American Curly."

"Don't know. Lemme take down your name and

number, darlin'. He's not answering his walkie or cell phone. He could be in the can."

I cringed. "Thanks." I gave him my info and said, "Could you have him call me ASAP? I'd really appreciate it. Thank you." My phone rang within ten minutes, but it felt like an eternity.

As soon as I said hello, a man with a thick southern accent said, "What's this now about a horse?"

So weird. He didn't even ask if I was the person who called.

"Um, I'm working with a white Curly ..." I stopped and corrected myself, "*American* Curly. She was in your circus two years ago."

"What about her now?"

"Do you remember her?"

"Honey, there's so many comin' in and out, I just don't know."

"Why would a horse not work out? She's calm. She's sweet. She doesn't spook at loud noises."

"Too stinkin' small or stubborn, I reckon."

"No, she's not stubborn, no way. But she is on the small side. She looks like a unicorn. Do you rememb—"

"Look. I kinda recall a white horse like that we snagged up real cheap about four years ago, and we did sell her. Not sure what to tell ya. Got no time for this. I gotsta get back to work."

"I just wanna know—"

"Can't answer anything more. Sorry."

"She's on your site though. To be sure it's her, you can look her up in the—"

"Can't. I'm busy. Like I said, size is the most likely reason."

"Where do you get your horses?"

"Usually the auction, but can't say as I know 'bout yours for certain. But I know she would'a been a filly. We like to get 'em young because they're easier to train. Gotta go."

"Wait! Can you tell me if she can do tricks?" I huffed loudly when he hung up on me and cut me off. Well, that was clearly the most I was gonna get. It helped a little, kinda. I figured Angel was no older than six. At least I knew her not working out was most likely her size, but I still didn't know exactly where Angel had come from before that. Hmm. I know there's an American Bashkir Curly Registry and that the Curly community is pretty tight. Maybe they can tell me where she came from.

I looked up their page online and zipped them an email with the info I had, as well as a couple of the twenty-five pics of Angel I had on my phone. Now that Angel was gleamingly clean, I noticed a small black spot just under and next to the top of her tail. It seemed strange to see this sole marking on a nearly-pure, white horse, but maybe it was a distinct enough detail that could help someone at the registry identify her. So, I sent a pic of that too.

Hopefully I can get some answers. I'm not even gonna tell Kat or Emily either until I find something out 'cause I want them to see that *I'm* just as good at sniffing things out as they are. They're not the only sharp detectives in our club. It only took Emily, what? A few hours to discover Angel was in a circus? I'm *just* as awesome. And

I'm gonna prove it. If the registry doesn't work, then I'll just try something else. It's a little mystery I'm driven to solve. I really want and need to know where Angel came from. And I won't give up.

12

I was excited when Leese showed up at my dad's on Wednesday night. Her dad dropped her off right after I finished washing the dinner dishes.

After showing her the make-shift bedroom and pull-out couch I slept on when I stayed over, she, Tia and I sat down at the game table to organize and box up the fall decorations, as well as the letters and drawings for military, and to mount the decorated horse cutouts Tia came up with onto cardstock. Everything was everywhere, and it looked like a craft store had exploded. I was really impressed that all the Angels pulled together and did so much so fast. I swept the military letters together with some drawings and huffed when I saw Tia's. "This was a good try, but you have spelling errors. '*Freedom*' should have an o not a u."

"Taaaahhh, well that's *dumb*-dumb. It's got the 'uh' sound like 'bus'."

I shrugged. "Whatever. I wasn't the one who came up with it."

"And fighting has a 'gh'."

"A 'gh'? But that doesn't even make any sense!" she cried, followed by a growl.

"It's spelled f-i-g-h-t-i-n-g. You can't mail it like this. You need to rewrite it. Plus, you wrote really messy. I can barely read it. We're trying to be professional here. You don't have to rush. Take your time so you can get it neat." But the truth was, we *were* kind of in a rush. We had to get these boxes out, plus, we wanted to get our horseshoes done and the rest of Tia's pictures mounted.

"All right," Tia scoffed with an eye roll. She slowly dragged another paper out of the pile of blank ones and picked up a purple pencil like it was sheer agony to do so.

When Leese finished putting decorations in her box, I taped it up. "So, these are going to the women and children's shelter?"

"Yep. I already talked to the director, and they said they'd love for us to throw a harvest party for the kids. She said, not this weekend but the next if we can swing it. Either Saturday or Sunday is good."

"Well, Saturdays are a little hectic for me now that I'm taking care of Angel and trying to..." I cut myself off before I spilled the beans in front of Tia. I didn't really care if Leese knew my plan, but I didn't trust Tia to keep her yappy trap shut. I picked up with, "...ya know, help her look her best." I sealed my box for the kid's hospital. "But, check with Tory and Posh. They're the ones who are going to be doing the bulk of the work, and I don't know if they have a game or whatever to cheer for. I don't know when or where they do it. You have both their numbers?"

"Yes. I got 'em." Leese said, sneering. She wasn't exactly a fan of Tory's either.

"Tory's being a lot nicer, trust me. This is good. Her helping us. She hasn't said anything mean to me all week. You?"

"No," Leese groaned. "She's been nice. I just don't like people who are mean just for the fun of it, like it's a blood sport."

I didn't want to tell her that grief might be a big part of that. Not only did blabbing about it seem wrong, I also didn't wanna upset Tia who was now drawing a dinosaur at the bottom of her letter. "I know, same for me. But I'm *trying* to be more open-hearted because I don't always know what people are going through."

"Yeah. I get it. Don't worry. I'll call her. I'm really excited about having the party for the kids anyway. I can't wait for yours too. Seeing the horses again'll be so much fun."

"Horses?" Tia cried. "We're having your party in the barn? I didn't know that. I almost puked the other day."

"No, or, at least, I don't think so. It's just gonna be at the McKinley's. You don't have to go to the barn again. They have a bigger place. And it's so pretty there, with the leaves all turning bright colors."

"I sure hope not," Tia said. "P-U! Horses are smelly."

I couldn't really deny it. They sometimes were, like Angel when she showed up at Sunnybrook. I was so glad she was sparkling now and less likely to collect sneers.

Once she gets thicker, she'll look even more fantastic. "They're *sometimes* smelly, but that's why we groom them, and if needed, give them a bath. Why'd you draw a brontosaurus on your picture for the military?"

"It's a *brachiosaurus*," Tia said. "I heard brontosauruses weren't real."

"What does a dinosaur have to do with them?"

"I'm gonna say they're as big and mighty as that. Is 'mighty' spelled the same as 'fight', with the dumb 'gh'?"

"Yes. Okay. I've been thinking, and we can't really give the military our regular calling card because they already are angels, right? So we need something more appropriate." I went over to the desk and sat on the swivel chair with my fingers poised over my laptop ready to tap out brilliance, but it just wasn't there. "What should we write, Leese? Got any idea."

She thought for several seconds, tapping her lip with her index finger. "Hmm. Maybe something like, '*Thanks for being angels! Your willingness to serve inspires us to be angels too*'."

"Yeah, yeah, that's good. I like that. Wow. You came up with that quick." I typed it out on our template with the logo Kat designed. "I was worried, but it fits fine." I sent it to print. "We can give these to the firefighters too. When's Tory giving them the cookies? Did she say?"

"Think Sunday. I'm helping her and Posh make cookies."

"Okay. Maybe I will too. I can catch her at school before the weekend to give her the new cards." I picked up the sheet and ripped them along the perforations.

When they were all separated, I stuck one in the military box. "Ready, Tia?"

She handed me three new letters and they were a lot neater. I put them in a puffy envelope. I was glad I made her redo them, although she was still kind of miffed about that. Once our boxes were set, Leese and I used Mrs. M's hot glue gun and decorated our fifteen horseshoes. Mr. M and Posh's father let us have all the leftover spray paint they had in their garages or basements, so we only had to buy small cans of pink, purple and another black because the can we had was low.

We each took five to decorate, except for Posh, who was gonna wave her sparkly wand of paintastica magic on ten to twenty of them, depending on how many more Kat could scrounge up and scrub clean. Posh only had eight at the moment, and she showed me a Japanese cherry-blossom one at school that put mine to shame. It was so beautiful. I mean, she even had the tiny burgundy flecks on the white and pink petals. I've never seen anything like that at a show. It excited me that this could actually be a way to earn some good money to help others.

I just stuck beads on mine because I didn't want them to look lame by comparison. *My* painted cows would look more like manure. I'll leave the detailing to her.

Although we wanted an array of colors and looks, my favorite were the silver and gold ones. Beyond looking more extravagant, they also somehow looked luckier to me. Leese did hers in silver and gold too. And of course Tia's were all, yuck, hot pink.

We set all our horseshoes on newspaper on the floor to

let the glue dry. Ours weren't as elegant as Posh's, but we did a good job and they looked adorable. I had confidence they'd sell.

After we finished her horse pics, Tia went to bed in the living room, thank goodness, 'cause I didn't want her in here when we were trying to write a song. She'd be bugging me with every little thing.

The packages were ready to be delivered, which I'd do after school tomorrow. My mom'll bring me everywhere, and then drop me off at the farm so I can take care of Angel and help out with therapy.

Err, I had so much to do to get both Angel and Emily ready. I still have to ride Angel to make sure my plan is even a go. If not, I'll have to come up with another plan, because if she *can't* be ridden and that's the *real* reason she was sold by the circus rather than her size, then there's no way on earth Mrs. M will keep her. And *that*...will totally demolish me.

I handed Leese a notepad so we could work on a song next.

"What do you wanna sing about?" Leese asked.

"Well, since this'll be for the show, instead of a lullaby —oh my goodness, my heart went spastic just picturing myself—I was thinking we should write about horses."

"We could write about horses, but we should write something that kind of motivates people since that's our club's purpose. What do you care about most, besides horses?"

I thought about it for two seconds and said, "Well, people being nice. I hate it when people are mean just because they can be. They often don't even care that you get hurt. And it's not just with words. Emily gets hurt by getting snubbed and ignored all the time. People pass her over because she's in a chair or on crutches. I want to make people stop and take a look and think about how their words and actions can be like knives."

She nodded and scribbled some stuff. "I really like this. We can work with this. It comes from a place of pain that we can spin into something inspirational."

"Yes. That's it exactly."

"Do you want to sing directly to the listener? As you?"

"Yes."

"So basically you're thinking as a line, '*When you see me, all you see is*' what?"

"You're asking me?" When she nodded, I shrugged. "The outside. But there's so much more to me."

She tacked on, "*Than what you see.*"

"Yes. That's great," I said.

"That can be our first verse."

"Just that?"

"Yep. I like it."

I picked up my guitar and hummed a few different bars. I went for slow and melodic, it seemed right.

"What happens when you're prejudged just like I am?"

"Well, I cry a lot, way too much. It makes me feel so broken."

"That's a good chorus lead-in. '*I cry when I'm broken*'. What else do you do that others do?"

"*I sigh when I'm so moved. I sing when I'm lifted into the sky.*"

She laughed and said, "See? Ha. I knew there was a lyricist in there. This is good stuff."

"You really think so? You're the one helping me string my thoughts together."

"Maybe. But it's good. Put some music to it now. Let me hear."

I put it to song, very quietly under my breath, and fumbled around to find a good and solid groove. I added, "*I crash when I'm so tired* ... um, um, oh, ... *I hide when I'm terrified.*" I lifted up on the syllable "ri" and it sounded nice, even as a whisper.

"I can't hear you."

"I know. I'm just trying to work it out." Once it sounded great to my ear, I raised my voice to let her hear what I came up with.

"Pretty voice! You shouldn't hide it. How about, '*I don't think*—hold out the 'think' for three beats—*you realize the depths of me. If you did ... if you'd stop to look. Then you'd see ... that I'm just like you.*"

"Sweet. I love that!" I screeched. When I worked that into the end of the chorus, I tacked on, "*I'm just like you-ou-ou ... just like you,*" at the end. It was stupendous.

"Awesome. Awesome. I love it! It's super amazing."

"I love it too. Now I need a little piece in there about Emily. I want to surprise her at the show."

We cranked out some more. My second verse had a couple more syllables, so I monkeyed around with the first to get them to match and added a third verse. Once we pieced it all together, and I ironed out the melody, we celebrated our teamwork with some topping-loaded ice cream. I really only have sweets on special occasions, and *this* was definitely special ... and beyond fantastic!

Eek! I was still leaf-jittery to share this in front of an audience, but at least it was my song and it would totally come from the heart.

13

After dropping off all the Angels' Kiss boxes, I was so thrilled to see Angel when my mom pulled up the long rocky driveway at Sunnybrook, I forgot to close the car door.

"*Mija!* Door!" my mom cried.

"Sorry, Mami." I blew her a kiss. "Love ya bunches! Bye. See ya later." I waved and took off like bees were chasing me.

I ran into Angel's barn and I'm sure she heard me coming because her head was poking out of the stall. "Hi, pretty girl. Wow. Even within just a couple days, you're looking a lot perkier. I really think you're putting on some visible pounds." When I put her halter on and led her out of her stall, her hips didn't look as bony to me. She was so extra-special gorgeous. *I* thought so, anyway.

I groomed her quickly because I was anxious to see what she knew and could do. I saddled her up for the round pen at lightning speed. And again, she let me put the bridle on without a hassle.

When I walked her out of the barn, lunge whip in hand, a diesel truck drove right by us and the driver honked his horn to let Mr. M know he was here.

Even at the extra loud noise, Angel didn't jump or back up. Nothing bothered her. She was the calmest, sweetest horse I'd ever been around.

However, she did react when she saw Emily's mom helping her out of the van and into her chair. Angel's whinny of hello carried through the sunshine and she bobbed her head as if repeatedly saying yes.

I waved and cried out, "Hi, Em! You're just in time to see me work with Angel in the round pen. Come on. I know you'll love it. We can see if she knows any tricks."

She zipped over to us, screeching a thousand hellos. "Cool. I can't wait." When she pulled to a stop in front of Angel, Angel bent her head down so Emily could stroke her. "Hi, Angel. You look so pretty. Did ya ride her yet?"

"No, not yet, but I did saddle her up, and she seemed very eager for a rider, so I don't think I can resist much longer. I just wanted her to be a little stronger. But I think, even in just a few days, she's really improved a lot. I'd maybe like to try today, if she does well following my commands, or before my party tomorrow."

"Oh, I'll bet she has improved. Can you give me a cookie to give to her later? I don't know where to buy them and my brother ate all the apples on me."

"Are you kidding me? You're talking to a horse junkie here. I always have cookies." I winked at her and pulled a handful out of my pocket for her. "See?" *One* wouldn't be enough with this girl. Even if she didn't offer them all to Angel, she'll want to give some to Ginger too when she sees her.

Her eyes twinkled as they widened and her smile grew when I handed it to her.

"Put it in your palm and hold it out flat."

"I know, I know. You know I've fed horses before. And I already gave her the mint. Remember?"

"Oh, yep. I forgot you're turning into an expert like Kat and me."

She smiled big.

Angel took the horse cookie from her hand platter, and Emily giggled when Angel licked her palm, looking for more crumbs.

"Come on. Let's go work with this loveable, huggable cupcake." I waved her to follow.

Em, the girl with a million questions, had already asked what a round pen was used for, and I explained that it was where we trained and worked with our horses.

"What's that for?" she said, pointing to the training tool in my hand.

"It's a lunge whip, and it's what we call a driving aid. We don't slap a horse with it. We mainly snap the ground or the air with it. It's like an extension of our hand."

"Oh, I got scared 'cause I thought you were gonna whack her with it."

"I'd never do that!" I was shocked to hear Em say that, because I'd never hurt a horse, but then, I remembered she was just learning about horses.

"Yup, Angel will move in the way or direction I want her to go. To understand better, just watch what I do. I'll use the lunge whip to move her into a walk, trot, or canter, and she should be able to turn in both directions when I shift my position and slap the lunge whip."

"And how does that help?" As usual one question with Em always leads to another.

"Well, it helps get the horse to focus on the trainer and lets the trainer understand what the horse needs and how much it knows. You become like a herd leader and the horse should focus on you."

"I get it," Em said, riveted on my every word. "She won't freak out with a saddle on?"

"Nope. I already tacked her up on Monday and walked her into the round pen. She was awesome and followed all my commands. No bucking or anything. I'll test more cues today. " I led Angel into the round pen that was beside the smaller barn where Angel was currently stabled. Kat was there waiting for us, and Emily followed me inside.

She was still full of questions and comments. She was becoming a walking, talking book, or I should say a *wheeling*, talking book. Every chance she gets, she tells us what she's learned, now that she'd been bitten by the horse bug.

"Oh, guess what! I learned a new word today," Emily said. "*Dressage.* It's a competitive equestrian sport that focuses on precision movements."

"I know. I compete in that," Kat said. "Sassy and I have won some competitions. She's so naturally regal, it's ridic. But enough already with the defs, Em." She huffed. "It's gettin' old. I'm sure you've told us a million by now."

"I know," she groaned. "Sorry for being a pest. I'm just so excited to have a new passion that actually comes up in conversation with other kids. I wanna know as much as you guys. I wanna be able to identify every breed of horse that exists."

"That's fine and great, but we need to work here," Kat said.

I was more interested in learning about how to train horses in general. It fascinated me, how you could totally turn a horse around. Working just this short time with Angel has given me a deep desire to train more. I've made up my mind. When I grow up, I want to be a real trainer and someday own my own farm that takes in rescues.

Kat led Angel into the center of the round pen and then walked back to stand next to Emily and watch.

I snapped the lunge whip in the air. Angel moved off toward the edge of the pen and began to walk. I let her complete a full circle, snapped it again and said, "Trot." Angel immediately went into a trot.

"Yay," Em yelled from the sidelines, clapping her hands. "Now I see how you do it."

Angel moved so smoothly and dropped her head beautifully, just like a well-trained horse would do.

Kat was watching intently. "Hey, check it, Jacinda! She's gaited."

"What's that?" asked Em

"That means she's not choppy in her trot," I said.

"She's as smooth-as-glass to ride, just like Sassy. Perfect for you, Em."

"I can't wait to get on her!" Emily cried with another clap of her hands.

I ran to the front of Angel to change her direction and sure enough she turned and trotted the other way. Without hesitation, she just kept on going.

"Ask her for a canter," yelled Kat.

I snapped the whip and yelled, "Canter!" Sure enough, Angel moved into a flawless canter. I let her canter around the pen for at least five times, and then yelled, "Trot!" again. Angel went back into a trot, and then I yelled, "Walk!"

"Cool, so cool!" Em cried.

Angel slowed right down into a steady walk, and then I yelled, "Whoa!" She stopped and turned to face me. I walked over and rubbed my hand down her side and gave her a horse treat and told her what a good girl she was.

"Wow, that's a surprise," Kat said with bug eyes.

"I knew she could do it!" Emily chirped excitedly. "She's perfect. When can I ride her?"

"Stop already," Kat said. "Not until Jacinda and I have. You're not near ready."

"When *will* I be ready?" she pleaded

I could see Kat was getting exasperated, but she held back her frustration and said, "When you can ride Ginger alone for a whole lesson."

"I'm doing that today," Em said with a determined voice.

"Okay then," Kat replied. "We'll see after that."

Kat, Emily and I had watched all the circus horse videos we could find, but each circus used different cues for different tricks, so that wasn't going to work for us.

It was up to us to try everything and see what Angel could do.

"Now onto the tricks. There are different things we can try." I swung my hand down, motioned for her to bow or lay down but she just stood there. "Rats."

"Does she follow commands for anyone or is it just the person who trains her?" Em asked.

"Not sure. Good question. Let's try something else." I swung my hand side-to-side to see if she'd shuffle one way or another. Again, Angel didn't budge. I could feel the stiffness sliding up my back in anxiety. I so badly wanted this to work. I wanted Angel's awesomeness to bowl Mrs. M over.

"How about a foot cross?" Emily said. "I saw people doing that with a horse. Try that. Stand next to her and move your leg in front of the other one."

I stood next to Angel with my shoulder against her withers and swung my left leg in front of the right. She copied me and nickered like she was laughing at me for taking so long to finally get one right. I slapped my lips as I laughed in astonishment. "Huh! It worked! Did ya see that?"

"Yay! She did it!" Em screeched.

"Hmph. Whatevs. Sassy can do that," Kat said smugly.

"If she can follow this one, then she must have other moves in there. We just have to find the right cues. I saw a shoulder tap in a video, so I'll try that," I said with a shrug of doubt. I did it with my hand and then swooped it down, but that didn't work either. I did the same thing with the lunge whip instead, and sure enough, she bent her knee and then dropped onto her leg. She lowered her head and did a bow. "A bow! Oh my goodness. Sweet. She remembers!" I just stood there in amazement, my mouth agape that it actually worked.

Emily began cheering and clapping and Kat held her hand over her mouth, with her eyes still trying to grow into suns.

"Haha! Bet your regal, precious Sassy can't do this," I bragged. "Not such a disaster now, is she?" Angel got up from her bow when I waved her up with a, "Stand," and she stood quietly beside me. I gave her another horse cookie and hugged her. "Good girl. What a great job."

Kat folded her arms and scowled at me. "Whatever. Ya got lucky."

"Nope. See? She's the smartest horse in the world!" I jumped up and down. "Told you she wasn't a mere Dirt Digger."

I could see curiosity and excitement blossoming in her blue eyes. "Wonder what happens when you do the same on her rump. Try that. You said some circus horses can drop down on the ground for the rider to mount. If she can do that, well, well, my mind will officially be blown."

I smiled and stepped closer to Angel, then reached over her with my lunge whip and tapped her on top of her rump. Sure enough, Angel dropped to her knees and then lay down.

I made an explosion sound and splayed my fingers at

the demise of Kat's snark and Emily cracked up. What could she say about Angel now? "Ha. Take that! How's that dynamite, AKA *crow,* taste, little kitty?" I started jumping up and down and screaming and it didn't even alarm Angel. "Yes, yes, yes! *That's* the move that'll win her a spot here. I know it. Oh my gosh, oh my gosh. That's it! That's what we'll use with Emily during the fundraiser."

Kat was won over. Now we were all hooting and hollering. I walked in front of Angel and lifted the reins. She got up, shook herself off and stood patiently waiting for the next command.

"I wanna ride her," Em shouted. She looked ready to jump out of her wheelchair.

"Not today, Em. If she's okay for us, you'll be next. We can work on it tomorrow."

Em's sad face said how heartbroken and disappointed she was.

"Come on, Em. You haven't had enough lessons for us to be sure you can do this. We'll test Angel out first and you can watch us. Then, once we're sure she can handle different riders, we'll let you try. Okay?" Kat was trying to make Em understand that she was not ready to ride Angel.

"Okay. But I know I can do it *now.*"

I knew we wouldn't be able to keep her from riding Angel for too long, with her I-can-do-anything-you-can-do attitude. Maybe it's from being physically challenged and wanting to prove that she can do anything a kid who can walk without crutches can do.

"We'll have you ready to show your stuff for the event.

Your mom and dad'll be so surprised. Kat, think your mom'll keep Angel for the program once she sees Emily ride, plus all her amazing tricks?"

"It *might* work, but we have to sneak and be careful no one sees us. Mom will *not* like us taking a chance with Emily."

I could see the determination in Emily's eyes. She was on a mission and that mission was to ride Angel and surprise her parents. "Yahoo! I can't wait. When are you guys gonna ride Angel?"

"Tomorrow, before my party," I said as I walked Angel out of the round pen. "I really think Angel's ready for a rider test. She actually *wants* to be ridden, which is so cool. A lot of horses lose their love and ease for carrying a rider if they aren't habitually ridden."

"I can't wait!" Em said.

"Me neither," I agreed. A bouquet of heart balloons with 'hope' written on them flooded my heart. I really, really prayed they wouldn't all get popped.

14

This was gonna be the most perfect day ever. I was finally gonna ride Angel, plus have my birthday party at the place I loved most in the world.

Right after school, I rode my bike as fast as I could to the farm.

I could see Kat already in Angel's barn. I dropped my bike on the ground. "Hi," I said as I raced by b her on my way to the tack room to grab a saddle, saddle pad, and bridle. Kat had put Angel's halter on and had her ready to walk to the round pen.

"She's good to go," Kat yelled back. "Meet ya there."

I heard Emily's wheelchair rounding the corner. Her mother dropped her off to spend time with us before the party. Kat and I were now Em's best friends, and her mother was really happy to have her not only interested in riding but in helping us train Angel.

When she wheeled in, I said, "Hi. Glad you're here!

Can you carry the bridle and blanket on your lap? I've got the saddle."

"Sure. Just put them on my lap," she said in her excited chirpy voice. "Can't wait to see you and Kat ride Angel, and then, I'll be next."

"Hold on, Em. We really do have to see how she does before you try to ride."

"I *know*. You already said that. I wanna try today *if* she's good for you guys. I've made up my mind. I can do it!"

"Aaaahh, I don't know. Your balance is better, but I don't know if you need more lessons."

Big fat tears started running down her cheeks as she looked pleadingly at me. "I don't! Please, pleaaaaaase. If you wait until next week's lessons, I'll only have two more weeks before the show. I can do it. I promise."

"Okay. Maybe." I couldn't stand to see the tears dropping onto her chin and listen to the last dragged out 'please' so I said what my mom always says to me to get me to stop nagging. "We'll see."

When we got to the round pen, I sat the saddle down, opened the gate, and took the tack from Emily.

Kat had Angel standing at the rail, ready to be saddled. Angel was a dream, standing patiently while I put the extra-thick saddle pad on and blanket and situated the saddle on her back. I pulled the cinch tight. Kat took off Angel's halter and put the bridle on. She took the bit in her mouth like an angel and looked at me with her puddle-brown eyes as if to say, "Let's go. I'm ready."

Even though she was still underweight, with her

sparkling white coat, Angel looked like she'd popped right out of a mystical dream or fantasy painting. Her thick mane, fetlocks and long forelock rippled like fluffy white marshmallow in the wind.

I set the stirrups to my leg length and Kat went to stand next to Emily. Putting one foot in the stirrup, I swung myself up and onto the saddle. Again, Angel stood calmly. I could already tell she was probably the best-trained horse I'd ever ridden. I was so excited to finally ride her, I felt delirious in my glee. I just sat for a moment, relishing the seat and sweet beast beneath me. I leaned over, wrapped my arms around her neck and gave her a hug. "Love you."

"Wow, I hate to admit it," said Kat. "But she looks beautiful under saddle. She's one flashy mare."

"Bye bye, river rat," I said.

Emily could hardly control her happiness. "Yay, Angel! You're so beautiful and you look just like a unicorn in one of my books."

"I know. She's stunning." I sat up, squeezed both legs and gave a cluck, and Angel moved forward into a walk. "Walk on, Angel. Come on. You're such a good girl. Look at you."

Her ears turned towards my voice and I knew she was paying attention to my every word. After walking her around the pen several times, I squeezed one leg and gave the command to trot. Sure enough, she did and we trotted smoothly around the pen. Kat and Em stared and said nothing. They were just watching our Angel horse move like a pro.

"I just have to say, this is the best day *ever.*" I beamed when I stopped Angel right next to Kat. "I love this horse so much, just in case you can't tell."

"No kidding." She ran her hand down Angel's side and praised her.

Emily shouted her glee. It was gonna be impossible to hold her back from wanting to ride.

Kat said, "Let me on. I wanna see how she moves for me."

"I guess," I groaned teasingly with a smile. "But you know I'm feeling greedy. Don't want to get off." I huffed in mock annoyance, jumped down from the saddle, and gave Kat the reins. She adjusted the stirrups and climbed up with the grace of a dancer. When Kat squeezed her legs, Angel moved off.

Kat's big smile said she was enjoying the ride, and now I could see for myself how gorgeous Angel looked under saddle. Tears came to my eyes, and I realized how much I'd fallen in love with this scrawny mare in such a short time. I couldn't wait for her to gain some fat on her body to show her full beauty. And yet, I was dreadful of exactly that because having her healthy will most likely rip her away from me. Kat put Angel into a canter, and she pranced so pretty. Nothing bothered her. Then Kat brought her to a stop in front of Em and me.

Giggling, Emily held her hand out with a cookie, which Angel quickly ate. She rubbed Angel's nose and kissed it.

"Kay, Jacinda. I've gotta get to cleaning stalls in the big barn with my mom," Kat said. "Thanks a bunch for letting me ride. She's all yours."

I frowned. I'd absolutely love it if she were *truly* all mine. But she's not. I rode Angel in the round pen for another ten minutes. With all of Emily's begging, I finally caved. I had to let these two connect as horse and rider. "Okay, okay. A *quick* ride. But don't tell anyone. Remember, this is a secret. I could get in big, big trouble for this." I looked over my shoulder to make sure no one was watching and put my riding helmet on Emily, then I tapped Angel's rump with the lunge whip and she got down in the dirt. Emily moved her chair closer, bent forward out of it, and gripped the saddle horn.

My neck, so on fire, was attacked with a poison-ivy itch. The smaller barn shielded the pen from where people were, but I turned my head over my shoulder to look again to make sure no one had stepped past it. We were in the clear.

I helped Em get situated on the saddle. "I should've done this while Kat was still here. You haven't ridden this horse before, so I hope you can hold your balance all on your own because I'm gonna be leading."

"I swear. I can do it, I can do it," Emily promised me with frustration laced in her voice because I didn't trust her. "You *know* I rode alone yesterday. I did the whole lesson by myself."

"I know, but she's getting up here. I'd think this same thing with any new rider, not just you. I'll stay right beside you as Angel rises because I don't want you to fall."

"I won't fall. I promise." She shrilled, "Eeek, I'm so excited."

"Shhhh. Keep your voice down. I don't want to draw attention over here."

"Oops. Sorry, Jacinda."

I handed her the reins. "Hold the saddle horn too, just for now, okay? I don't know how this is going to go."

"Yep, yep," she chirped and bounced in the saddle seat. "I got this. Don't forget I'm using my crutches more all the time. They say at rehab, even just the few lessons of horseback riding has given me more strength and lots of balance and they can see the difference. It won't be any time at all and I'll be strong enough to get out of this wheelchair forever." Her eyes had a determined squint. Though I once doubted it to be true, now I knew Emily will do anything she sets her mind to. She was actually a lot stronger than me.

Standing next to her with my hand on her thigh, I waved my free hand up towards the sky beside Angel's eye, motioning for her to rise. "Stand, Angel." I feared she'd lumber on the way up to her hooves with someone on her back because she still didn't have much meat on her, but she got up gracefully on all fours like she was only wearing a cloud. Emily's smile was so big, I feared she'd scream in delight again.

I put my index finger over my lips to remind her to be quiet. "You're good up there?"

She nodded insistently like she desperately wanted a second cupcake at a party. "Definitely. This is so amazing. I feel like a princess."

"You look like one too."

"I do?" she said, astonished.

"Yep. With your red curls flowing in the wind. Remember to keep your voice down, okay?"

"Okay. Don't worry."

Yeah. '*Worry*' owned me. I looked around again. My racing heart thumped in my ears as I adjusted her stirrups. I wiped the sheen of sweat off my forehead and took the lead line in hand. I led Angel around the pen. They both were doing great. I only let Em ride a couple minutes though because the whole time I was terrified of getting caught. I didn't want us to get into trouble. This was a huge no-no. I mean, I could lose my job here, and that would crush me. But so would losing Angel. Getting these two ready to show off their stuff was the one thing that could keep Angel here. I had to take the risk.

Emily was sad to get off and back into her chair, but she smiled when I told her she'd get more opportunities than anyone else to ride Angel, including me. She felt better at that and the fact that I'd printed out one of my pictures of Angel on a sticker that she could put on her chair.

"Oh my gosh, thank you, Jacinda." She actually teared up when I pulled it out of my back pocket and handed it to her. "That was the sweetest thing. It's *your* birthday. You shouldn't be the one giving presents." She didn't even care that it was a little curled.

"Ah, don't worry about it. You've been such a great friend and you love Angel as much as I do."

"Hopefully, we can make her as *stuck* here as this sticker."

Okay, now I was the one tearing up. "Yeah, hopefully. At least we know Angel can be ridden and even lay down to pick up a rider. That's her best shot of scoring a home at Sunnybrook. In conversations I've had with Mrs. M, it's clear she sees her as a toss-away. She's looking forward to the money she'll bring into the program. Because she knows tricks, that only adds to her value, and someone'll want to buy her more. And my whole plan could backfire. But I'm hoping, things'll swing the other way, and Mrs. M's heart will melt when she sees how much good Angel can do here."

"Let's not show *all* her tricks then, just enough to make a strong impression."

"Good point. Let's not. It'll be so crushing to lose her."

"Yeah, tell me about it." I had Emily open the gate for me, and I hopped up on Angel and rode her back to the barn to take her saddle and bridle off. She was so perfect. I gave her a cookie for doing such a good job, removed her tack, and turned her out to eat some sweet grass and enjoy her day. Angel's friend Ginger was waiting for her and gave a friendly whinny. Angel whinnied back, the way horses do. She pranced her way to Ginger, and I could tell she was proud of all the work she'd done today. Angel was the most amazing mare in the world.

Now I knew for sure, she had a high chance to stay in this place where sunlight glistens and shimmers on the winding brook. That was my only birthday wish. And I'd close my eyes tighter than ever when I blew out my candles. I don't know if being fervent and passionate helps win over the good graces of the birthday fairy, but I'll give it a shot anyway. It couldn't hurt.

15

I was so psyched for my party at Sunnybrook. Mami could not have picked a more amazing spot, and lovely Angel was gonna be the highlight of the afternoon.

After closing Angel in her stall, I started skipping over towards the gazebo in Kat's backyard where people were already clustering. *Stop, skipping. Idiot! You look crazy.* I smiled huge when I saw the bouquets of white and purple balloons reaching for the sky and all the white Christmas lights twinkling around the posts. I bet that was Kat's idea, with the sun so close to setting. I jogged the rest of the way and spotted my birthday cake with chocolate frosting. A white frosting horse was drawn on top, and the mane and tail even had swirls like I've described Angel to just about anyone who will listen to my bubblegum pop. My mom totally nailed it!

Even though we weren't rich, Mami always tried to make every birthday special for me, and this was gonna be the best one yet. All my anxiety over who to invite seemed ridiculous now. I actually looked forward to spending time with friends. Yes! I truly have friends! Finally. I had my party all planned out in my mind. First, we'll have the pizza, cake and ice cream, and then, we'll tour the barns again, and I'll bring Angel out for everyone to meet. They saw her in her stall on Sunday, but now, they'll get to see her in her full glory and pet her silky, wavy coat.

I asked that no one give me presents. Any price of a gift should be donated to our club. We desperately needed money for supplies to create our treasures and desserts to sell.

So I was butterfly-happy but laughing to see that Tia put out the jar like I asked, even though it said, *Donuts for Kisses*, rather than *donations for kisses*. Then again, maybe she does want the donuts. The Heavenly Seven agreed and said they'd do the same for their birthdays.

"Thank you, Mrs. M for allowing my party to be here. That was so sweet."

"No problem, Jacinda. It's been a pleasure having you here. I don't have to worry about you, even though you're so young. You behave responsibly and always do the right thing."

Feeling a dart of guilt, I looked at Emily and cringed slightly because that wasn't entirely true *today* with me sneaking Emily onto Angel's saddle. Kat didn't even know about that yet, unless Emily told her while I was walking to the barn. "Well, I ... *try*."

"You've done a fabulous job with Angel," she added.

"She'll command a pretty penny I'm sure, once she's gained a bit more weight."

Yeah, way to jab me on my birthday, lady. "Surely," I muttered with a frown. "Who wouldn't want a horse as glorious as she is?" Quickly changing the subject so I wouldn't cry in front of everyone, I said, "I'm thinking of doing rescue when I'm older. I really love it."

"I'd love to do that too," Kat said. "We have the same dream."

"I bet you both would be good at that," Leese said.

"They already are," Mrs. M said, giving us props.

"Hey, Jacinda, are we gonna ride today?" Emily asked.

I shrugged and said, "I don't know. It's up to Mrs. M. Can we?"

"I certainly don't mind. We can take the short trail. Are you up for that, Emily?"

"Yes!" she cried with a fierce arm cross and scowl. She clearly hated being called out and put in a different category than the other girls, especially those that had never ridden.

Her mother chastised her for being rude.

"Well ... I can do it, Mom," she insisted.

"No way am *I* riding," Tory said. "Horses are nasty and smelly."

"That's what I said," Tia said. "I can't stand horses. I have to see their flared noses and big, goofy teeth every day when I'm playing dolls on my bed."

"They aren't smelly or nasty with sudsy baths," Emily said. "I've helped out with that. And it's not a big bubble bath if that's what you're thinking."

"Thanks for clarifying," Posh said with a laugh. "That's what I pictured."

I guess, Kat, Em and I were the only horse-crazy kids in the group and that we weren't going to ride. Bummer. We had a great time anyway, laughing and chowing down pizza. When it was time to blow out the candles and cut the cake, I wished Angel would *please, pretty please*, get to stay and that our booth would be a great success for us and that we'd raise mega bucks to fund more Angels' kisses. We were having fun, but I was anxious to bring all the girls to the barn again to show off Angel's tricks. I was determined to prove that horses weren't disgusting slobs.

Papi, happy for the night off, stayed behind with Mami and Mrs. M to clean up and talk, and all seven of us ran, squealing, to the barn. Emily was right behind in her wheelchair. I asked if anyone wanted to take a ride on Ginger in the round pen, but no one changed their minds.

The minute Angel heard Em's wheelchair, she let out a loud nicker. "Angel, Angel," Em yelled. She sure did love that horse. And Angel loved her. Everyone gathered around Angel's stall. Her head was already poking out for snuggles and craved attention. I pulled a horse treat out of my pocket and she lifted it from my palm.

The girls were just watching. They hadn't been around horses that much.

"Can I feed her one?" asked Tory.

"What happened to '*nasty*'?"

She shrugged. "I don't know. They're not so bad I guess. Especially *this* one."

"I know. That's why she's our club's namesake. She's a

gem. Just hold your hand out flat like this." I gave Tory a treat and she held her hand out and Angel gently took it from her.

"Oh my word," she said with a laugh as she looked at her empty hand in amazement. "That's the first time I've fed a horse. And she didn't bite me."

"She's so beautiful, she gleams," said Posh.

"I know," Emily said. "I dream about her."

Rubbing her hand down Angel's side, Kat added, "The wavy coat and curls everywhere, even inside her ears, are traits of an American Curly."

"They *know-oh*. *I* told them all about that before," Em said.

"Oh, right," Kat said. "Forgot."

"Horses, horses, horses," Tia said with a wrinkled nose. "Blah. That's all Jacinda talks about, but I guess she *is* a little pretty."

"So, this is the horse you want your parents to keep, Kat?" asked Tory.

"Yup. Jacinda, Em, and I have been working with her every spare minute. We know she'd be perfect for the program. You should'a seen her when she first got here. She was the yuckiest, dirtiest, skinniest wreck imaginable."

"She doesn't look that way now," Posh said as she gently touched Angel's nose.

"Thank goodness Jacinda saw potential in her, because I sure didn't." Kat picked up Angel's halter. "We'll take her out so you can get a better look. Step back, guys, so I can let her out. I'll put her halter on and Jacinda can *really* introduce her. You only saw her briefly before."

"She's won you over now, hasn't she, Kat?" I said with a snicker.

"Maybe. Now that I've seen what she can do. And she's not such a disaster anymore."

"Well, I love, love, LOVE her," Em said, craning her neck to see in-between everyone standing by the stall.

"Yeah, like that's *not* obvious," Kat muttered.

I elbowed her to shut up.

"So, whose horse is she really?" Leese asked.

"Angel's Jacinda's project horse," Kat said, opening the stall door. The girls moved back, afraid to stand too close. "But she's no one's really."

I hated the sound of that. Even though it was true, it hit me a punch to the gut.

"What's a project horse?" Tory asked, stepping behind Em's wheelchair.

"It's a horse that's rescued for some reason or other. We call it a project horse when one person or two work with it. Some people do that to save a horse's life. It may just be cleaning and then riding it, but mainly it takes a lot of love to work." Kat slipped the halter over Angel's head.

"And I was here when Jacinda volunteered to take Angel on. Someday I'm gonna get a project horse of my own to take care of. Right, Jacinda?" Emily looked at me with the question.

"Sure, Em. If you work hard enough, you can do anything. Kat and I know you can." I caught Posh rolling her eyes like she didn't believe it and Leese's jaw dropped open. But they didn't know Emily like I do. I just smiled, knowing she'll likely do anything she sets her mind to.

"Whoa, she looks so big," exclaimed my imp.

"She's smaller than all the horses here actually so that's why she'll make a great therapy horse. They help disabled or mentally challenged kids and adults, even those with emotional issues, like people with depression or returning vets with post-traumatic stress."

"Yeah, people like me," Em chirped.

"How does it *help* though?" asked Posh. "I don't get it."

Deciding to let everyone brush her so they could see just how much of an angel she was, I walked Angel to the crossties and everyone followed. I clipped Angel in on both sides and Kat went to get brushes to hand out. "People begin with learning how to groom and care for a horse, and then move on to riding if they're able. Most, but not all, can eventually ride. Working with a large animal like a horse builds self-confidence. If you're brave enough to work with a horse, you can face obstacles in everyday life."

"And you meet new friends," Em added as she wheeled to the front of Angel and gave her another treat.

"And it's just plain fun," Kat said, coming back. She handed each girl a brush.

"What if a kid can't sit alone?" asked Leese.

"That was me at first," Em said as she moved her chair to the side of Angel and took a brush from Kat. "I was terrified of being up so high, but I had a side-walker and Jacinda led Ginger for me until I felt ready to do it alone. Some kids need two side-walkers."

"Did it take long for you to begin riding alone?" asked Tory.

"Nope. Only two lessons. And the doctors said my balance and strength have improved so much just from the little bit I've already done. My mom's thrilled to watch me ride Ginger all by myself."

"When you watch a horse move," I said, "you'll notice that the rider kind of rocks in the saddle. The movement is very relaxing and helps with balance. That's one of the main things kids with disabilities need to work on. Horses move with a certain rocking rhythm. It's kind of like when we walk, except many of our kids can't walk so they get the feeling of walking when riding. This moves muscles and increases flexibility."

"Cool. You know everything. I'm impressed," said Tory, as she stroked Angel's side.

"Thanks for the compliment," I said. "But really, I only learned all about it since I've been volunteering. I listen, watch, and read *any*thing about horse therapy."

"How can I be a volunteer?" Tory inquired. "I know I don't know much about horses, for sure, and don't think I want to ride, but I love helping kids."

"Me too," said Posh. "I might wanna ride them someday though. Maybe. A small one like Angel."

My heart melted. Who would've guessed the person I most feared was so kind? "Just let Mrs. M know. She'll put you to work."

I felt suddenly so proud of what I do as a volunteer. To be honest, I volunteered to be around horses, but I ended up gaining so much more from the kids in the program."

"Are all the horses gentle like her?" asked Posh.

"Yep. They gotta be. It takes a special horse to be in our program," Kat said, checking out one of Angel's hooves.

"Is it expensive?" Posh asked. "There are some autistic kids in my cousin's section of town who could benefit from therapy, but their parents can barely afford food. It can help autistic kids too, right?"

"Yeah, definitely," Kat said. "We have a few. Some kids are able to get partial or full sponsorships. *That*, plus the costs for horse care and other operational expenses *depends* on donations and sponsorships, which is why we have the annual fundraiser. We also do other things throughout the year to raise money."

Posh said, "Wow, cool, I never realized programs like this existed. It's so amazing."

Kat explained, "All our help is volunteers. Everyone's like family too and we work hard to make the kids the best they can be. Wait 'til you see them at the event. It's such a blast. They're so excited to ride and show what they've learned. Some still need side-walkers and some can ride alone, like Em."

A big smile bloomed on Emily's face.

"Yup," I said. "The program focuses on what the kids *can* do, not what they can't. Some kids can never mount a horse but love the experience of grooming. It doesn't matter. They find comfort and independence and that builds lots of self-esteem."

"Although I've never been around horses, I love Angel," said Tory. "I can see why you think she's special."

Emily nodded. "She is. She's my friend. I loved horses before I started here, but wasn't sure about riding. My mom thought it might help my balance and give me strength, so she brought me here to try it. Thankfully, Jacinda helped me get over my fear. I'm gonna encourage other kids in wheelchairs to do this too."

"Kids can learn a lot from you, Em. You'd be a great volunteer," I said, backing her up.

I'm sure they saw Emily in new light as she rattled off information about circus horses and how Angel used to be one and knows a bunch of tricks.

They cheered when I showed them what Angel could do.

I never in a million years would've thought my arch nemesis, of all people, would not only be at my party but asking questions about what I'm most passionate about. I also didn't expect that doing good deeds would be changing my own heart as well. Even in just a few days, it truly felt bigger. I couldn't wait to see how much money we could raise at our tent because there were so many things I wanted to do, so many ways I craved to help others. I wanted to cry in frustration because we were somewhat stunted in what we could get done. We couldn't really do a whole lot with only a fistful of bills. Hopefully all our treasures will be a big hit ... and Angel too.

16

I had a busy Saturday taking care of Angel and getting
Emily ready to ride in the show. She rode Angel
without me leading this time and did great. I gave Angel
another sudsy bath to have her all gleaming for the
coming week. Hopefully, she wouldn't dirt dive. She
hadn't yet, although, I did see her cutely rolling in the
grass.

When I woke up Sunday morning, I was hoping an
email had come in from The American Bashkir Curly
Registry because it had been a week already. I was kinda
bummed to find nothing. I guess it wasn't a *huge* deal that
I didn't know where Angel had come from before the
circus because whatever her past, it hadn't affected her in
a negative way. She was still as sweet as pumpkin pie. But
I was just hoping to dig up something on my own to
impress Kat and Em. I know I'm just as good as them
in finding things. I did see a breeder page when I was

hunting for info about American Curly horses, so I zinged a couple emails to them as well. It couldn't hurt.

I got dressed and my mom dropped me off at Tory's house to help her bake cookies for the town firefighters. Although they were volunteers, some were always on duty, so I'm sure they'd appreciate the thoughtful gift and yummy treat.

Kat was at church, Tia *hated* to bake and went to our neighbor's house instead, and Emily had a baby shower to attend, so it was just me, Tory, Leese, and Posh. Her house was jaw-droppingly huge. It was seriously a McMansion. I rang the bell, turned and waved to my mom and a man answered the door. He introduced himself as her dad.

Mirror image, curved staircases met me in the marble-floored foyer when I entered at his wave to enter. After bombing a joke, her dad told me to go under the balcony and turn to the left. With my mouth agape, I'm sure I was gawking in wonder like a prisoner who'd been released after serving a twenty-year sentence. I spun around, taking everything in, and lifted my chin so I could check out the ritzy chandelier with a gazillion sparkling crystals. No wonder Tory acted haughty more often than not.

Hearing all my Angels, I knew I was the last to arrive. I followed the echoes to the kitchen, which made mine look like a mouse hole, even though it was actually wicked big, I thought. Mixing bowls with dry ingredients already sat on the counter.

Three out of four of the girls waved to me and, without even a hello, Tory immediately ordered me to wash my hands with a point to the sink before I touched anything and "germified it" like I was some idiot baby or a garden troll who'd just come in from digging for onions. "I know," I sang irritatedly with a sneer. "Thanks." I slid my jacket off and put it on a kitchen chair.

"No!" Tory cried. "That should go on the coat rack." She had wild, I-just-sniffed-catnip eyes, like the stress of baking was driving her nuts. What on earth? I thought she liked to bake!

"Well, no one told me."

"I just did."

"Fine." When I was turned away, I mouthed, "Wow," to myself. I hung up my coat on a black iron coat rack beside a door that I'm guessing opened to the garage. I walked to the sink and scrubbed my hands with the grapefruit liquid soap that was there. The sweet citrusy scent tickled my nose. Once I towel-dried them, I spun to find Tory glaring. "What."

"You're late! We have a lot to do. Cookies. Meals for two new moms. I signed us up."

"I *know*, sorry. My sister hid all my shoes. She's a little imp who plays annoying pranks on me all the time. I looked all over and couldn't find anything. That's why I have these dumb sandals on even though it's kind of chilly today."

"Our party at the shelter is gonna be next Sunday, but it's at noon. That's the best time they said. Right, Leese?

"Yep."

"So, here's what we're gonna do. Make Italian cookies for the party today too. We won't have time to make them later."

"Won't they be gross?" I asked.

"No, duh, of course they won't be gross. They need to dry out for a couple of days."

I caught Leese shaking her head side to side in annoyance, which almost made me laugh. I bit my lip and shrugged. "Oh, well, I wouldn't know."

"That's right. That's why *I'm* in charge here."

"You do know what you're doing. So, um, just tell us what to do."

"Okay. Everyone, listen up. We need to each take different tasks. Leese, you can cut up the chocolate bars into chunks and melt them down in a saucepan. That'll be a dip for some of the cookies. Jacinda, once I have the ingredients mixed for the chocolate chunk cookies, you can scoop the mixture onto the cookie sheets there."

"Sure, I can at least scoop. I'm sure I won't screw *that* up."

"Even a monkey can scoop."

I crossed my arms with a sneer and cried, "Hey! Are you saying I'm no better than a monkey?"

"No, I am just saying … it's a simple job. For you."

Okay, that definitely didn't dissolve the slam. I was still wearing a capuchin tag around my neck.

"Posh, I have the ingredients all measured out. Mix the butter, lemon zest, and vanilla first. Then add the sugar and eggs, one at a time, after each one is mixed through. Baking powder is already in the flour, so you just have to add that white-powder bowl in next, but don't over mix it. Then we can pipe the dough out."

We got going on our tasks, but she barked at Leese,

"No. Turn the flame down! You're gonna scorch the chocolate!"

"Thanks, oh mighty one," Leese snapped with a turn of the dial. "That's why we have you, for your precious, infinite wisdom. You didn't have to be so abrupt about it."

"I don't even know what you're talking about."

"Not surprising. You're all cotton candy up there." Leese pointed to Tory's head.

"And you're so stinking weird! At least you're quiet and hardly speak."

Leese turned away from the burner with a huff and took a step closer to Tory. She was seething, with her nostrils flaring and fists clenched tight. "Maybe, I just don't like talking to snobs. Ever think of that?"

Tory's face said she was boiling more than the chocolate on the stovetop. "Listen, *chica*, don't you *dare* get in *my* face. I will kick you into the gutter so fast."

"Go for it," Leese said, moving closer to Tory. "In *this* neighborhood, it's probably made with gold."

"Hey, hey, ladies, let's all chill out, okay?" Posh said with an arm block to keep them separated before a real catfight broke out with claws and everything.

"Right," I said, backing her up. "We're supposed to be doing good deeds here, not fighting with one another. Let's just get back to cooking." Okay, I maybe should have anticipated some head butting with such varied personalities in one cluster, but because of how well things were going, I just assumed it would be pure bliss. Wrong! I was totally gobsmacked by this.

"Whatever, Miss Bossy," Tory said, looking at *me*.

"Excuse me?" I said, all wavy in annoyance. "You're the one barking at everyone. Quit it. You need to just relax."

"Don't tell me what to do!"

"Take a page out of your own notepad and follow it," I insisted. "That's all *you've* been doing since I walked in."

"*I* am the culinary expert in this group and *I* know how to do things right. I don't want you bumble heads screwing it up. That will reflect poorly on me. I always do my best."

"We are *trying* to do our best," Posh said, "but you don't have to be so rude to everyone."

We were all huffing mad when we returned to our tasks in silence. At least, I thought it was silence before Tory interrupted my scooping with another slam.

"No, Jacinda! You need a much bigger scoop than that. How would you like to eat dry, burnt pebbles that are *supposed* to be cookies?"

"Okay! All right! Just say it nicely next time. How's this?" I said, sticking on a bigger glob.

"Better. I just want everything to be perfect."

"Fine. I want that too. Can we all be cool now and get back to work?" Wow, cooking with her was a complete nightmare. She was like a drill sergeant, and she didn't really let up. I just took it as her crummy leadership style. It wasn't at all pretty, but we put up with it and it worked, leaving us with the best-looking chocolate-chunk and Italian cookies ever. Some of the golden treasures were crowned with chocolate, as well as rainbow sprinkles or tiny, pearly white balls. Some had coconut or a dot of oven-safe jam. A few were left plain and they still looked pretty and scrumptious. The baking of cookies made her kitchen smell heavenly.

She remembered to put our card with the chocolate chunk cookies in the brown bakery box. They were set on a doily and sealed up with a crisscross of purple ribbon. She ripped the loose strands through the press of her finger and a scissor's blade, turning them into bouncy ringlets.

Her mom dropped us off at the mall, and we dashed to the fire station first before going to the mall to look for craft supplies with my new birthday money.

Posh had a container of freshly squeezed lemonade in a back pack, and Tory did the same with the box of cookies. We wrote a note with a fat black marker and stuck the note on top of the box, that said, 'Thanks for being heroes in our community! Enjoy the cookies & lemonade! Your Angel Friends.'

We set our goodies down, rang a bell on a side door, and took off running in a fit of laughter. We hid behind a bush and watched to make sure someone picked up our kiss right away.

A lady in uniform answered the door, looked down and saw our gift and checked out the area. She took our gifts inside. We high-fived each other and Leese gave me a hug.

"Aww. I hope they love it. I'm sorry I was such a bossy brat, guys," Tory said. "I just wanted everything to get done right."

We went back to the mall to get craft supplies and watched a lame movie as a breather while there. It was supposed to be a comedy, but I didn't laugh once. Maybe because I was distracted by everything that happened today. I just stressed and stressed and was left with a jumbo, tangled knot in my chest.

While waiting outside the theater in the back of the mall for Tory's mother, I said, "Guys, we really need to get along better."

"Don't be annoying then," Tory said.

"Now, *that's* just what I mean. Words hurt. We can't have anyone attacking anyone else. It defeats the purpose of why we're doing this."

"I know," Leese said. "Sorry, I came at you like that, Tory. I just don't fully trust you yet."

"Yeah, I kinda have a bad rep, don't I?" Tory said. "I'm gonna work on that."

I certainly hope so. I scowled and clutched my icky stomach. My precious club felt splintered and so at-risk of falling apart. I really didn't need this kind of headache right before the fundraiser! I thought finding a way to get Angel to stay was my biggest concern, along with raising money, and now, I feared my sweet dreams for the Heavenly Seven could blast up into tiny chunks from the hard smash of a wrecking ball.

17

On Monday I rushed to the farm to work with Angel, but Kat caught me by the arm to show me what she was working on.

"Come on! You gotta see what I found." She jumped up a couple times and waved for me to follow. "This is so sweet." Without even looking back to see if I was trailing behind, she took off running towards the old off-house garage that was just used for storage. "These were in here and not being used, and my mom said we could have 'em?"

I just saw old lattices. "For what?"

"For our booth, duh? Use your imagination, Jace. They look a little weathered now, yeah, I know, but I'll paint 'em white, brace the back and tack nails in. Then, ta da, we can hang our horseshoes for display. I'm already attaching the string, wire or thin rope to all the horseshoes we've already done. See?" She opened a box and shoved a horseshoe into my chest. "Check it out."

I shook my head in disbelief. "Wow, Kat, this is fantastic." I seized the hot pink horseshoe Tia had painted and pulled it forward to get a better look. I thought they would look butt-ugly in this color, but Kat attached a peacock feather, some braided rawhide strings that crisscrossed again and again from one end to the other, and glued on a cluster of turquoise beads. It looked so cool. "You even made these hot pink ones look good. I can't believe it." I looked in the box.

"I hope you don't mind my extra embellishments. A few of them needed a little more oomph."

"No, not at all." She took the most boring designs and made them stunners of beauty. A white one had silk flowers and ribbons. It looked perfect for a wedding. A tiger striped one had some black beads that decreased in size from a swirly, exotic bead in the middle that looked like it held a gray tornado in darkened sky. "These look so pretty. I just know we'll sell a ton of these. How much do you think we should charge?"

"We have fifty-three in all. I asked my mom and she should said we could charge ten bucks because they're so pretty. My mom is gonna spot us a $100 in broken bills for making change. Tory *insists* on handling the dessert sales."

"Good. Let her have it."

"I'm tag-teaming with Leese on some poem cards. I'm gonna paint around her calligraphy and mount them. Tia's pictures are kind of cute, but I don't know if they're worth ten bucks. Do you think she'll be mad if we charge five for those?"

"Nah. She'll just be glad we're selling the thing she

came up with. What about, Em? Everyone's doing something their passionate about. I don't want her to get left out."

"She won't be!" Kat said with a beaming smile. "Check it, she already told me she's making pinwheels for kids in wheelchairs or on crutches, so that people will be more inclined to look at them with something catching their eye. She's making them as free treasures though, as an angelic gift of kindness."

I had to press my fist to my eyes because it choked me up and made my throat feel scratchy. I was seriously on the brink of sobbing when I said, "Wow. Fab idea. She came up with that?"

"Yep."

I coughed to clear the tickle and catch my composure. "She's such a bundle of determination and joy. She impresses me more and more every day."

"I know. I admit, she's the cutest thing, even though," Kat's voice began to drag, "she won't shut uuuup about horses. I don't mind a little, but it's non-stop. How'd the baking go? "

"Total disaster. A major fight broke out."

She laughed and swooped her fist in an arc. "What? Really? Aaww, I miss all the good stuff. Was it all hockey-brawl-like and bloody? I would've taken bets."

"It was internally bloody. It makes me question everything about the club. We're supposed to be working together doing good deeds, not tearing each others' hair out."

"You can take some of mine!" She yanked at her

ponytail. "Speaking of hair, this wild, frizzy bush is such a nightmare. Luckily, Posh stopped by to drop off more horseshoes and gave me a hair gloss to try. I hope it works."

"Even if it doesn't, you still look button-cute."

"I'm about button-sized too."

I laughed.

Kat walked with me to the barn so we could work with Angel and make sure she had the cues down cold. I didn't want any glitches.

Angel moved like a dream. She bowed, did a leg cross and got down on the ground with a grace you often don't see in everyday horses. She definitely belonged here. I just needed to prove it.

"Emily's coming extra early on Thursday before her lesson," Kat said.

"Good, then hopefully, we can find a way to sneak Emily on again without anyone knowing."

"Next time, make sure I'm there. That was so crazy."

"I know. But she rocked it."

I helped Emily clean a senior lady's kitchen and bathroom on Wednesday before going over to my dad's. Em met her at the senior center. We worked very quickly as a team, and she accomplished so much more than I expected. Because it was a narrow kitchen, she was able to lean back against the counter and mop the whole floor. The lady, Gladys, was so sweet and fed us meatballs. My dad usually makes me supper so I ate only three so I wouldn't be stuffed. Although Emily was excited to have tackled such a big task, she was even more ecstatic to be riding Angel when she showed up at Sunnybrook on Thursday before her lesson. I had to shush her and remind her not to squeal or shake her fists.

Once I had Angel bridled and saddled up, I led her to the round pen with Emily wheeling behind me.

She was clapping.

"We gotta wait for Kat," I said, then shushed her with my index finger over my puckered lips.

"Why?"

"It's just safer with two people. Someone'll need to keep a lookout. We don't want anyone to find out what we're doing."

"Okay. That makes sense."

"Hi, guys," Kat said with a perky voice. *Too* perky.

"Planning something evil?" I asked, suspicious.

"Noooo, I'm just really excited to get this party started."

"Me too," Emily said. "I can get on Angel now?"

"Yep. And, at the show, she'll prance in looking all gorgeous. And then surprise! She'll drop down, stunning everyone, and you'll mount, and she'll get up with you in the saddle."

"Oh my goodness," Kat said, "I can just picture it now and how amazed the crowd'll be. So cool."

I tapped Angel for her to drop down for Em.

Emily wheeled up to her, gripped the saddle horn and got up onto the saddle by herself. I checked to make sure her boots were properly in the stirrups.

She took the reins and gave me a thumbs up.

I stood in front of Angel and said, "Stand, Angel."

When she did, Emily hooted.

"Shh, Em," Kat said, dribbling a basketball that wasn't there.

"Okay. Right, right. I'll be quiet as a mouse. I promise." Emily clicked her tongue and Angel started walking around the pen. "Can I trot? I wanna move faster!"

"No, Em. Be happy to just *walk* Angel. That's good enough for now. After the big event, you can try a trot with her. You've got to promise me you won't do anything but *walk* when you are on Angel, and *doubly* promise for when you ride in the event. "

"I *pinkie* promise."

With Kat on lookout duty, I let Em ride for a few more minutes, and she was talking to Angel the whole time. She said, "Whoa," and Angel halted. Emily bent to give her a neck hug.

Kat suddenly started waving furiously at me. My stomach dropped. "It's my mom. Hurry! Stop right now," she shouted in a whisper.

"Lay down, Angel," I said, and bopped her rump.

She did it on command, but before I could help Emily off, Mrs. M was there staring at us, her hands on the rail. "What are you girls doing?"

"You know Angel's been so good and sweet," Emily said. "She doesn't spook at all, not even with the big trucks. So I promised Jacinda all my popcorn jellybeans to let me sit on her."

My heart never beat so fast. It was drumming faster

than the jazz I've heard. And I'm pretty sure the world started crumbling all around me.

"Doesn't she look so pretty on Angel, Mom?" Kat said, turning my way. Her eyes widened and looked close to exploding. I could see a cord of tension in her neck.

Em snorted and crunched back a laugh behind her curled lips. Yeah, *she* can laugh! It wasn't her volunteer job on the line.

"She'll just stay like that, lying down?" Mrs. M asked.

"Yes, Ma'am," I said.

"Well, even though she's sweet, I'd really like to keep Emily on the therapy horses, all right?"

"Awww, but I love Angel," Emily said, tearing up, her voice so shattered, it made me want to cry too.

"I know, honey," Mrs. M said, "but we really don't know all that this horse has been through or if anything will trigger her yet. For your safety, I'd really like you to stick with the horses I know. And you girls shouldn't get too attached. You all know she's a rescue and that this is just her temporary home."

"I *know* that, Mrs. M," I said with tears in my eyes.

She tilted her head, looking at me with pity. There might have been a hint of compassion in there, but it was mostly pity.

Kat and I helped Emily back into her chair. And Emily wiped her eyes and bent down to pet Angel who remained on the ground.

"Love you, Angel. I really hope it works," Emily muttered.

"What works?" Mrs. M asked, her eyebrow perked.

What on earth, Emily! I gritted my teeth. *You're gonna ruin everything!*

She sat up and said, "All the, ya know, work Jacinda's been doing to get her ready for a home of her own."

I was holding my breath and finally exhaled, impressed that she came up with a good answer that wasn't even exactly a fib.

"I'm sure it will. She's looking amazing to me," Mrs. M said. "You've taken really good care of her, Jacinda. You too, Kat. You girls should be proud. She's doing great and putting on the pounds now. Are you ready for your lesson, Em? Miss Carol's waiting for you. And Ginger's all saddled up and ready to go." Mrs. M came around the pen to open the gate for her.

"Good. I have cookies for her too."

"I know she'll love that. You're penciled in for lead with Miss Jane, Jacinda. Tommy should be here shortly."

"Okay. Thanks." I handed Kat Angel's lead line. "Will you turn her out for me?"

"Sure."

I walked away from Angel, and the world was still crumbling around me.

18

Our parents were so proud of the work we were doing with our club. The Angels had a busy week doing good deeds. Though there was some snippiness from the tension of rushing to accomplish a lot, no more fights broke out. Maybe everything would be okay. I hoped.

We raked elderly neighbors' leaves. Emily did more internet training at the senior center. Kat and I got all the therapy kids to sign and leave hand prints on our big sign for Mrs. M. Timmy, one of the cerebral palsy kids, couldn't uncurl his hands enough to get his palms flat, even with help, so he wanted to do his footprint instead. Em thought that was so adorable when she saw it. We also left sweet notes in various places for people to find, that *hopefully* made a difference. Kat and I taught Tia how to ride her bike without training wheels. We also spent time at the shelter on Saturday morning decorating the fellowship hall for the dance party we were throwing for the kids. And, to top it all off, Kat and I worked with Angel and Em. They were both doing great. Huuhh, so, with all that whirlwind activity, I was feeling totally zapped, and we weren't even finished yet! Even though doing angelic duties took a lot of hard work, all the good cheer we were spreading around like confetti and sparkly glitter made it well worth it.

Tory's kitchen was a madhouse now as everyone but Tia was cooking and prepping to get everything ready for the party tomorrow. At least we had a long weekend with Columbus Day off.

"We can't have all junk food and sweets," Kat said. "We have the Italian cookies. We can just make brownies from a box and that'll be good."

Tory gawked in shock. "We are *not* making brownies from a box! Nasty. Brownies are so much better from scratch."

"Fine!" Kat cried, with her fists clenched. "But you wanna do shortcake and cookie cups to hold M&Ms, *plus*, brownies and the cookies we already have? That's too much sweets."

"*I* want to do everything and…"

"She's right. This isn't a bake sale," Leese said, putting her two cents into the argument. "It's a party with little kids. And we want to be good examples."

"We can use the strawberries on a fruit platter instead," I said, "instead of cutting them up and sugarizing them for shortcake. And we can make a veggie platter."

"Little kids *hate* veggies," Tory cried. "Nice try, Jacinda."

"Not *all* little kids," Leese said.

"Tia *loves* veggies," I said, backing up my own point.

"The shortcake mix is already mixed! What are we gonna do with that, huh?"

"Maybe the Rescue Mission in Springfield'll take the shortcake," Leese offered as a branch of peace to help compromise.

"They won't," Posh insisted. "I called already to see what we could give once we get money, and they only take packaged food. Store cookies at most. They won't take anything homemade."

Tory stomped her foot. "I *don't* wanna *waste* the batter!"

"Make them for your family then!" Kat shouted

My neck started burning as the argument began to escalate.

"You gotta pick two desserts, Tor," Posh said glaring at Tory and backing Kat up. "I like the idea of fruit and veggie platters."

"It's gonna go to waste!" Tory shouted. "I'm telling you. I've done things with little kids before."

"We only have nine kids for this party," I said, steaming and feeling like my top was about to pop. "There's no need for us to create a giant feast, especially one with only sugary sweets."

Emily, who'd sat quiet the whole time, suddenly spoke up and cried, "Errr, stop fighting! Please! It's hurting my ears! I get what Tory's saying, guys. She doesn't want to waste the food we already started making. Let's just cook everything Tory wants to make, and we can create *one* dessert platter with a little bit of everything, and *then* a veggie and fruit platter. It's simple. We shouldn't be fighting like this. We *need* each other for this club to be its best. I hate everyone fighting like cats and dogs."

"You're right, Em." Posh said.

"And that's the perfect solution," I said. "Good thinking, Em."

"Yeah, I *am* good for some things," she said.

Kat bopped her arm. "What. You're good at a lot of things, like defusing bombs that are about to go off."

She laughed and we all laughed too at how ridiculous we were being, fighting over something lame like food.

We finished up, made our three platters and went to the center to finish getting the hall ready.

The next morning, we showed up earlier than the scheduled time so we could paint the girls' nails. There were six girls and three boys, all different ages.

The little blond girl whose nails I was painting stared at me like I had a booger on my nose. Every time I looked up from my task of swiping on pink, Gemma was there, meeting my eyes. "What do you want on top of the pink? My little sister likes pink. That's her over there." I pointed Tia out. "Posh over there with the cool braids can do just about any design you want." Although, maybe I shouldn't have said that. Gemma's nails were about the size of pomegranate seeds. They weren't big enough to hold much art. "Polka dots would be cute."

"No, then they'd look like ladybugs. I can't stand bugs."

"Not even ladybugs?"

"*No* bugs," she said through gritted teeth.

"Okay, okay. No bugs. Got it."

"I like plain pink." She was still miffed that I even suggested the dots. She reminded me of Tia.

Once all the girls were glammed up, we turned on music, but no one wanted to dance. We looked like fools. Emily cracked up. She was using just crutches today but currently wiggling in a chair to encourage people to move.

The boys were crossing their arms and saying they didn't want to do this dumb thing.

The costume pieces Posh found sat untouched in a trunk.

Posh sneered at me and whispered, "Not as cool as I hoped. Maybe not everyone appreciates Angels' kisses." She said to the mentor, "They don't wanna dance. What do we do? This is totally tanking."

"I don't know. We do plan some activities, but this is the first event planned by outsiders. Some of these kids have issues with trust."

She nodded. "Okay. I get it."

Then, Emily, out of the blue, just started talking about Angel and how she was my project horse. Her eyes lit up as she spoke about how disheveled and mangy she looked when she first got to the farm, and how she looks like a unicorn out of a fantasy novel now. She passed her phone around so people could see her. The kids oohed and aahed over her beauty. She also told them how scared she was to ride Ginger but overcame her fear and was riding all by herself now. Love that girl! Emily comes to the rescue once again! Her sweetness and openness loosened all the kids up, even the boys.

And when Posh started in on a cheer, they all wanted to learn it and the moves. Then we finally moved onto dancing, dressing up all silly, and having a total blast.

Leese, Posh and I showed up early at Mick's Bowl on our Monday off of school. We called ahead to let him know we wanted to record a song in the booth.

He unlocked the door for us and we went to work.

I wasn't sure which kind of cut Posh's brother would want to use, so I recorded two versions with just my voice while listening to guitar on headphones that I recorded on my PC and turned into an MP3. Then, I did two singing with the guitar. Lastly, I tracked out just the guitar parts. I had to pay $10 for the CD, and we thanked Mick for letting us in early.

We took the CD to Posh's brother, and he decided to use the separate tracks, and he then blended them with the keyboarded sections and beats he made.

I loved what he did with it. It enhanced everything I did. It took him just over an hour to mix and polish it up, but then he played it for us. The guitar wasn't cleanly captured in its original state, but he was able to take out the fuzz and make it crystal clear.

Leese was fanning herself. "Woo, we are *so* hot."

"I know. It came out so good," I said. I hugged Micah and kissed his cheek. "Thank you, thank you, thank you."

"Ah, no prob. It was a fun project to add beats to. The song wasn't too long or complex."

"We wrote another song, but didn't get to record it yet, short for time and all. Can you put this on CDs for me to sell at our booth? I can pay you back once our money comes in."

"Sure."

He played it for us one more time. And I *loved* it. I suddenly wondered if music therapy could help horses or if it was already in use. I definitely needed to learn more about that. That'd be the best thing ever, to use my very own talent to help project horses shine and become even more amazing. You know what? I'm *not* just some towering ogre or doo-doo brain who stayed back in third. I like ... rock!

19

Kat and I spent every secret minute on Thursdays and Saturdays helping Emily ride Angel and getting her ready to show off her tricks.

It's been hard keeping Emily's riding a secret, not only because Mrs. M was now on high alert but also because Emily was so proud of what she could do. She was about to bust a gut because she wanted to tell everyone so badly. Emily's parents will be thrilled to see how good a rider she is, and hopefully, the McKinleys will see that they can't let Angel go.

Mrs. M has watched Kat and me ride Angel all around the farm, and she's impressed with how far she's come, but she has no idea she can do tricks or that Emily can mount Angel all by herself. Emily rides Angel around the pen like a champ and is constantly begging to do more. We promised, again, to let her do more after the fundraiser.

Mrs. M has done an amazing job with the vendor

scheduling and making arrangements for the therapeutic riders for the big day. But that and getting the farm ready has kept her really busy, which gave us moments here and there where we could work with Emily and Angel. Now that Sunnybrook has had a few of these fundraisers, she's like a well-oiled machine. Hundreds of people were expected to attend, maybe thousands now, because it's getting so popular.

It was Friday night, the day before the big day, and knots and butterflies were wrestling to be the more prominent irritation in my stomach. I waved to Mr. M who was mowing the grass with the big tractor. The sweet scent of hacked grass welcomed me. I'm glad I don't have allergies because I love the scents of grass and hay. Our 10' x 20' tent was set up by the entrance, right beside the huge wooden banner that said, *Sunnybrook Farm Therapeutic Riding Center's Fall Fundraiser.* In smaller letters beneath the name was *Equestrian Show and Art Exhibit.*

All the Angels met at Kat's house so we could bake and finish all our crafts. We decided to put up most of our display tonight because tomorrow was going to be crazy and hectic for all of us.

"These came out so awesome," Emily said, checking out several of the horseshoes. She began to hang them on the lattice Kat had peppered with nails. She gave two claps. "Oooh, look how pretty they are."

"Everyone did an amazing job. I'm impressed," Posh said. "This booth will truly represent all of us." She was going to lay Tia's pictures out on our card table, but the breeze was determined to rip them all away.

Kat clapped her hands together to catch the one that somersaulted through the air.

"We'll have to wait 'til tomorrow to put these out," Tory said.

"Awww," Tia whined.

"If we put 'em out now," Posh snapped, "they won't be here by morning!"

"Hey! Don't yell at her," Tory said. "She's only six. She didn't know. She's just excited to put out her artwork."

Uh, not now. Not again. Another argument's the last thing I need. Great. Even these two besties were fighting.

Tia crossed her arms in a boastful stance and gave Posh a 'yeah' nod. "Yeah. You heard her. I'm *exciiiited.*"

"Fine!" Posh said, followed by a growl of defeat. "But like Tory said, we should *wait* 'til tomorrow. We can put 'em right up front on the table with the poem-pictures. How's that?"

"All right," Tia whined, giving in.

The tension that had coiled up in my neck and head began to unwind as the argument ended, but I really couldn't take something extra to worry about right now. Everything had to go perfectly at the fundraiser, and this was just stressing me out!

"Remember what I said yesterday," Emily pressed. "That we all need each other in order for this club to be its best. We need to find a way to get along, even if it seems impossible."

Leese was just standing there quietly at the other lattice, minding her own business but likely steaming about the flaring attitudes. Yep. She turned to me and gave me an eye roll.

Kat spotted that and cracked up while she was busy poking Emily's pinwheels into a foam tower. "I'm not saying anything."

"For *once*," I joked.

Kat laughed again.

Leese said, "Since we're not using the tent flaps, do you think we should put our horseshoes, facing out, like a wall? We can put them right up front."

"No, the food needs to go up front, with the price sign," Tory said. "Everyone wants to know where the food is."

"Look!" Leese spat. "These horseshoes are our big seller. *This* is what is going to make us money for our club not your dumb food that other vendors are going to have."

I was getting so stressed. "Hey, hey. *Please* don't fight," I yelled. "Cut it out, everyone! We *need* to get along. Please!"

"No, stop arguing," Emily said, coming to the rescue. "Look. I got an idea that'll help with both things. We can use the horseshoe lattices up front, but as side walls." She used her hands to motion where she meant. "That way every time people walk or drive in or come down the dirt driveway, the horseshoes'll be the first thing they'll see."

"I love it," I said. I looked around. Smiles were spreading. Everyone liked the idea too.

"And then," Em continued, "we can use tables up front for the baked goods on one side and Tia's pictures. We can also put the Need Box on the food table where it'll be noticed. And because our tent is so big, we can also do

L-shapes with two tables on each side, creating a path in between that invites people into our tent to check out our stuff."

"Right," Posh said. "I like that idea. We have so many great things to sell, and that'll give people a chance to see things up close. We can put the third wall of horseshoes inside our tent at the back, facing out, so people coming into our booth can see them."

"Like Leese's poems," Em said. "If we do the L-shapes it'll give us a lot of table space to display stuff."

"Or my horse pictures," Tia cried.

"Well, your horse pictures are on bright paper, making them stand out, and they'll be up front," Posh told her, "but the duo-coolness of Leese's poems and Kat's watercolor paintings are on pastel parchment, so we don't want them to get overlooked."

"Oh, I get it," Tia said with a nod. "What about Jacinda's CDs? Where are they going?"

"What CDs?" Kat cried. "What! You made a CD?"

"No, it's just—"

"And didn't tell me?" she screeched.

"It's *not* a *whole* CD. It's just a song that Leese and I wrote together. Posh's brother mixed it for me and it came out pretty good. I was *thinking* of selling it, for maybe $5 or something."

"After she sings," Tia said with a clap, "it'll be a big seller."

"Thanks for the vote of confidence, Teacup."

Kat huffed with a big grin. "So, you're actually doing it? You're gonna sing? Like, in *front* of people?"

"Yes, yes, yes she is," Tia said like the happy little snitch she is.

I shook my head and crossed my arms over my chest. "I guess." I looked at Emily and said, "I really want to...to prove I'm strong and brave like Em."

Emily's warm smile radiated all the way to China. "You think I'm strong and brave?"

"Very."

"Wow, that's the nicest thing anybody has ever said to me." She started to cry into her fist, and then I choked up too.

I bent to hug her. "Aww, don't cry. I love you, Em. Why are you crying?"

"I love you too. You guys are the first true friends I've ever had."

"You're *smart* too," Leese said.

"Thanks. I hate it when we fight."

Leese added, "You came up with the perfect solution to our problem."

I looked around, and everyone, even Tory had tears in their eyes. Emily was the most precious thing imaginable. I'm so lucky to have met her. "We'll try harder to get along, okay?

"You are our glue, Emily, and you know just how to defuse a tense situation," Leese said in her poetic way. "That's a talent too. That means you're a good mediator."

"I really like that," Em said with a nod. "Thank you."

We all hugged it out and vowed to do better at controlling our anger.

I wasn't entirely confident Angels Club was on

trajectory to Utopia. We'll see. With a bunch of girls, most competing to get their strong opinions across, that promise could be easily broken.

But, I can't wait to see how it all turns out! I have hope that everything'll go perfectly.

20

I was beyond excited for today's fall fundraiser. We were up and at 'em by six o'clock. No alarm needed for either Tia or me. We wolfed down our breakfast and dressed at break-neck speed. We had so much stuff to carry that Mami drove us to the barn.

The sunshine beaming down on me and Tia when we got out of Mami's car promised it could chase away the morning's chill. I so believed it, even if I didn't already know the forecast of sunny, partly cloudy and low 60's. I started out with a sweatshirt, let's just say, I was *forced* to wear a sweatshirt, even though I told Mami I didn't need it. She was volunteering today, so she'd know if I ditched it too soon. I love crisp, autumn days, the bite on my cheeks and the yummy scents, like at the farm which smelled like nutty-sweet leaves. The scent of freshly-mowed grass still lingered, even though the ground had been kissed by a thin layer of ice crystals.

"Mami said a million pieces need to fit together for this to be as successful as last year's and to beat last year's total amount gifted."

"Why do they need to get money?" Tia asked.

"It's expensive. Kat and I told you at my party how and why. There are more kids in need of the program now, and the McKinleys have brought in a few new ones, which is why Mrs. M doesn't really want to keep Angel. Horses are expensive. Some kids are on scholarships. This fundraiser can help support that, plus just the general operation of everything. People today can sign up to sponsor a horse or a kid ... or the program itself."

"Cool. I know I don't really like horses much, but Angel's not so bad. She *is* pretty. I hope she'll get to stay."

"I have a plan. Hopefully, it'll work."

"What's your plan?"

"You'll have to wait and see. You won't be able to miss it. You'll also get to see the rider's showcase, which, I'm told, is amazing." She and I passed the cider donut stand and took big whiffs with "aaaaahhhhs" on our exhales. I could smell cinnamon too. Yum, yum. This cart had donuts plus candy apples and cider. I might get one of each later. This also was certainly a special occasion where I might let myself enjoy the sweeter things in life.

I walked her over to the large field Mr. M mowed where some vendors were already setting up. Tents, boxes and people unpacking were everywhere and a lot of pickups were parked for unloading.

"It's so weird Mami's working here today too."

"No, not really. I think she and Mrs. M are becoming

really good friends. I can see it in their laughter and the way they work so well together. And besides, you know, Mami's the best helper person ever. She has such a compassionate heart." The whole farm was teeming with helpers and filled with a bustle of activity.

"See all this craziness? It takes a ton of people to set up and get ready for this. Mrs. M said by 9:30 or so, everything'll look amazing once all the goods are out."

"Uh, I'm glad we set up last night," she said, sounding exhausted just taking everything in.

"I know. Although we're by the entrance with the best spot, this is where the bulk of the people sell their stuff. There are a couple authors who write horse novels this year too. Mami will be helping Cheri over there." I pointed and waved, but she was busy talking to someone.

Tia started spinning around to take in all the sights. "It's so cool. It looks like a circus with the tents and decorations and striped, um … those things, whatever they're called."

"Canopies." That word '*circus*' made me smile but it made butterflies dance in my belly because I immediately thought of Angel and what we had planned for her and Emily. It just had to work! I looked up at the sky and said a silent prayer that everything would work out. What if Emily slipped or Angel spooked at the loud sounds and the cheering people? *No, don't think about it.*

"Ooo, *mira*! That one's got Italian ice. I love watermelon. Can I get some later?"

"Yeah, you can use the twenty bucks Mami gave you for anything you want."

"Cool."

I was in equal wonder looking around. "You're right. It does look like a circus. It's so colorful and bright. And *this* is only about a quarter of the vendors."

Huge coffee pots sat on a table for the vendors, along with bagels and donuts, and I watched as some of them walked by, paper cups in hand and huge smiles on their faces. Mrs. M said vendors love their coffee and that happy vendors make for a successful event. I can't wait to check everything out once it's all set up to see what goodies are for sale. Kat told me all about this event and how big it was, but I couldn't picture it. Now that I could see it with my own two eyes, I was amazed. I've been to all kinds of horse shows, but *this* was definitely the biggest.

I walked Tia over to our tent. Leese was already there. She had the light aqua table cloths on the four tables and was starting to put out her poems. It made Kat's watercolors pop. She had also turned them into greeting cards and had about ten bundles tied with ribbon.

"You did cards too?"

"That's a cool idea," Tia said.

"I helped someone create bundles like this for a birthday party and had leftovers."

"They're gorgeous!" I said, checking them out. "I like how everyone comes together with their talents to help Angels Club work."

"That's one of the best things, it's like sparkling magic." Leese looked up at me. "Well, it looks like we're the only vendor outside the arena area."

"I know. How cool," I said. "We got prime real estate."

Tia said with a grumpy whine, "I like *pink* tablecloths a whole lot better, but since you guys wouldn't go with that, this light blue is all right."

"Not everything can be *pink*, Tia," I said. "We need to compromise sometimes."

"Okay. I know." Tia went to her box and started putting her swivel-leg horse pictures on the front right table.

Mrs. M set up a pot of hot chocolate and cider donuts on a tea cart for us. "Aww, Mrs. M is so sweet. Who's taking care of the banner for her? I'll be busy…" I stopped, clamming my mouth shut, and looked at Tia, "working with the horses and riders for the showcase at noon."

"Posh is gonna handle that," Leese said. "I think she's having it presented at the showcase."

"Ah, good. I feel like I'm spinning around in two different ways like on the Spyder ride."

"Just relax. Drink some cocoa. Everything'll go great. Think positive."

"Uh, I'll try. Tory has the baked goods we bagged up? Did she take them home?"

"No, they're in the kitchen here."

I shrugged and sneered. "Should we wait for her to put them out?"

"No, no. Let's get 'em now!" Tia cried. "People are coming in. We want 'em to hit our table before they get to the donuts."

"She has a point," Leese said, followed up by a huff of despair. "As delicious as our goodies look, I'm not sure we can compete with donuts."

"Okay, how about we just put out the cookies and

brownies for now. When she comes with the tiers, she can set up the cupcakes. She's gonna want them in a perfect order."

"Kay."

"I can get the boxes in the kitchen," Tia insisted.

"You're sure?"

"Yes, I can do it." She darted off.

"Don't you dare drop 'em!" I yelled.

"I can't wait to see what the vendors are selling," Leese said.

"Me too. Kat says, by ten, the air will be filled with the smell of deliciousness."

Leese took a big whiff. "I can smell some of that right now."

Posh showed up looking amazing in her dark jeans and billow-sleeved blouse. Waving, she screeched, "Hi-ii, lovely ladies. I'm sooooo excited."

"So am I. Wanna help me hang our club banner?"

"Sure."

We unrolled it. "Wow. Kat did such a great job," I said. The huge red-lettered sign said 'ANGELS CLUB FUNDRAISER' at the top, and it had horseshoes and horses painted all over the sign. Leese and I stood on chairs and pinned the grommets to tabs that were already on the front of the tent when we took it out of the bag. We put the tent up with the help of Mr. and Mrs. M.

Kat must've been busy helping with other duties. She showed up with Emily wheeling beside her. Her hair was all glossy, straight and smooth today, with just her sides pulled back in a barrette, so I did a double take.

"Love your hair. You look fantastic."

"Thank you. Posh worked her magic on my disaster fuzz and showed me how to blow it out and straighten it."

Tia came back with the baked goods and Emily helped her arrange them on the left front table.

"What's Tory gonna charge?" Emily asked. "We'll have to make cards."

"She made a sign," Posh said. "Everything's a dollar."

"Works for me," I said. I unzipped my back pack and put my CDs next to Leese's pictures with a feeling of dread in the pit of my stomach.

She noticed my nausea. Maybe I was green. "Our song is great. Don't worry, Jacinda. People will love it."

"I guess. I hope so. This is kind of a trial run to see if it's worth it to do it for the babies."

"I think it is," Leese said. "Micah made them sound pretty close to pro."

I saw Emily grinning ear to ear. She was over the moon to ride Angel today. Kat and I have worked so hard with Angel and Em, and they are a team. Angel takes such good care of Em, and Em has been chomping at the bit to show everyone how she can ride and what a great therapeutic horse Angel is. I think Em's a natural on horseback. She has courage and loves horses, but most important, she wants to be the best she can be. I've learned in watching her to be grateful for what I have and to try harder at everything. If Em can do this, I can do anything, including, errr, sing, which I'm totally dreading. I feel like rocks have made a home in my stomach.

Tory finally showed up with her fancy cupcake tiers.

Emily put out the "What's Your Biggest Need" box. She decorated it with angel stickers. So cute.

Tia helped Tory get the cupcakes, and the rest of us worked to get all the pictures set out. All the horseshoes were hung last night and they gleamed on the wooden lattices in the sunlight, especially the silver and gold ones. Still my favorite.

People began to stop by, and we were on a roll, each doing our part to sell and stay happy. We really needed our booth to bring in the most money possible, and we had so many varied things to sell, I believed it would be a huge success. With our growing list of people to help, we'll need every penny to do our good deeds. We're the Heavenly Seven and, for now anyway, we were united and excited to make it happen. We were so happy with our club and our team effort.

Even though Tory griped a little about us setting up the treats before she arrived, her skills were vital to our club's success. We'll just have to deal with scratchiness and assume we won't always get along with one another, which is okay. That'll only make us stronger. I hope. But most importantly, Tory was totally done with bullying me, and even acts like she likes me … well, most of the time.

Kat took a few of the girls to show them the arena.

Chairs were set up against one wall for the guests, and tables with ribbons of different colors to give to the riders sat off to the side. Each rider will receive a ribbon and the kids were very excited to show off what they've learned. They've been practicing for weeks and the instructors were very happy with their progress.

But the big surprise for everyone will be when we walk into the arena with Angel and Emily.

All of the staff and the McKinleys think I'm gonna walk Angel out into the ring and introduce her as my project horse. Just wait 'til they see Angel drop down and Em swing onto the saddle. Picturing it made me want to do a little dance. It's gonna be so awesome! Almost time. Eeek.

21

Fifteen kids signed up to ride today and Miss Jane, Miss Carol, Miss Mary, and Mrs. M were working to get all of the horses tacked and ready to go. Mr. M was also helping with the horses and lots of their friends, including my mom, will hand out awards and let people know where to sit. After the kids ride, attendees will tour the barns and have a chance to visit the vendors again or go to the donation table and help sponsor a rider or give a gift to help the program.

Kat and I left Tory, Posh, Leese, and Tia to finish setting up the table so we could jazz up the horses and riders. Emily was with the other kids, already watching the horses get groomed and decorated with colorful ribbons. Mrs. M was excited to show how much our kids have learned and how far they've come with balance and courage. Mrs. M loves what she does and has a special place in her heart for our riders with disabilities.

She's especially impressed with Emily, who rides Ginger by herself and balances beautifully.

Although Mrs. M's impressed with Angel, I think she's showing her off today in hopes of a sale.

All the horses have colored streamers threaded through their manes and tails. They look beautiful. Ginger looked adorbs with the pretty blue streamers I put on her. Kat beautified Sassy with bright yellow. But just wait 'til everyone sees Angel! She truly looks like a magical white unicorn. I threaded multi-colored streamers through her mane and a large bow sits above her tail, with long streamers hanging down. Her mane is long and curly, and her white forelock hangs between her eyes, giving her a mystical look. I swear she sparkles when she moves. We have a large blue string of small bells hanging from her neck, and when she moves, she sounds like part of a fairytale. We've tested the bells on Angel while Em was riding, and as usual, she was totally cool with even the jingling. She actually looked like she enjoyed the tinkling and lifted her legs a little higher. She was so well-trained by the circus with all its blaring sounds, loud music, and cheers, that nothing startled her. Plus, she was always extra calm with Emily on her back.

The kids looked so cute, dressed in western boots and cowboy hats. Many of their family members were taking photos of them standing or sitting next to their favorite steeds. The air buzzed with excitement and everyone was anxious to get into the arena.

Emily wore a pink shirt, a white skirt with pink fringe, and pink floral western boots. A white cowgirl hat decorated with a pink, floral band sat on top of her red curly hair, completing her outfit. She looked so adorable that I don't think anyone will even notice the scars from her many surgeries that run up and down her tiny legs. What people will definitely not miss is her special spirit and determination. Those things shine like sparklers in the night.

By noon, the arena was packed. Many people brought fold-up chairs of their own, which was so good 'cause early birds had already filled the set-up chairs an hour ago. My stomach felt jittery and Kat said she felt the same way. The only calm and steady one was Emily. She had the steel in her eyes that she gets when she's determined to do something that someone says she can't.

The other Angels were busy at the booth, but they'll come in right before the show. Some teen volunteers said they'd watch our booth so everyone can see. Not that I didn't trust them, but we made $280 just in two hours, and for safe keeping, we put the money away in Kat's house. After the show, Kat, Em and I will stay at the booth so the girls can scout out the other booths.

The riders showcase was about to start and I could hardly wait. Eeek. My palms tingled and my heart pounded out a tribal beat. Hopefully, our surprise will work, and Mrs. M will realize what a great therapy horse Angel would be for Sunnybrook.

In this arena of horse lovers though, I knew she'd get offers when everyone sees how beautiful and talented Angel is. That was my biggest fear: that all our hard work will backfire and Angel will still be trailered off to some other farm because the glossy price tag will be too much for Mrs. M to pass up. She does have a deep love for special, sweet horses though. That's what I'm resting all my hopes and dreams for Angel on. Maybe she'll fall in love just like we have. I hope. Dread whirled up into a vortex in my stomach. I waved to the Angels as they stood along the sidelines.

"Jacinda, you're next," Mrs. M said as she walked one of the horses out of the ring. I was standing with Star, a brown pony one of our younger kids was sitting on.

Emily was next after me, leading Ginger in her wheelchair. She asked Mrs. M if she could lead instead of ride today because she wasn't sure about riding in front of so many people.

"Okay, Mrs. M," I said as I signaled Kat.

I led Star around the ring, and Timmy, the one riding her, hooted in celebration. I smiled and tears built up in my eyes when everyone clapped and cheered for him. I waved to the crowd.

After several circles, he whined, "Aww, can I do one more? I have fans."

I laughed and said, "Sure." Having never been to one of these, I didn't know if that was against the rules, but Mrs. M gave me a thumbs up when she saw what he wanted to do.

I waved Emily to go next. She was beaming so huge and about to burst out of her cowgirl boots.

When I passed her, she cried, "Walk, Ginger," and led the brown mare with the lead line. I was surprised she made two circles so gracefully, and I was even further surprised to hear Em shout, "Trot." She laughed and laughed as she sped around in her chair.

I smiled and stood stunned when Ginger trotted beautifully beside her.

Even though she was gonna ride Angel, she was really making the most of this. Then, I suddenly realized what she was doing. She was showing kids in wheelchairs who might be present that even if they could never ride, they could still have fun with horses.

Miss Jane was surprised too and gasped. Her eyes bugged out in astonishment.

Kat shrugged and said, "Hey, what'd you expect? She's an eager learner and pretty stubborn once she gets an idea in her head."

"Why do I get the feeling you girls had something to do with this?"

"Don't look at me. I'm just as shocked she called, 'Trot,' as you are," said Kat. "But then again, it's not really *that* surprising. If you knew Em like I do, you'd totally get it."

Once she circled it three times, she called out, "Walk." The horse went into a steady walk, following her lead around the ring. Then she said, "Whoa," in the middle of the arena. She turned her chair around, kissed Ginger's nose and gave her a horse cookie. "Good girl. You did a great job."

She loudly said, "Walk," as she rolled back to the entrance of the ring where she stopped at the gate.

Kat was holding Angel's lead line, waiting for me to walk her into the center of the arena. We were the last ones on the agenda, and as I said, I thought it was because

Mrs. M wanted everyone to see our beautiful Angel with hopes of a buyer. Emily handed Ginger's lead line to Miss Carol and waited for my signal so she could wheel over and mount Angel when she dropped down.

Mrs. M took the microphone in hand, announcing the end of the show and thanking everyone for coming. She praised the volunteers for doing a great job and introduced everyone. She also thanked everyone for their donations and support. People stood and applauded and cheered so loudly I thought the roof would collapse. The show was a grand success and now, *now*, it was *our* turn. They haven't seen anything yet!

The local television station was filming, and I saw a newspaper person talking to one of the kids while a photographer was snapping pictures.

Mrs. M pointed to me and said, "Now I'd like to introduce Jacinda and Angel. Angel, an American Curly and rescue, has been Jacinda's project horse. Jacinda's not only given her the best care, but she's ridden her and put in tons of extra time to work with her. My daughter, Kat, has also helped with Angel. Angel's a mare who never fails to amaze us with how much she knows, how much she's learned, and how willing she is to please. She'll make an amazing horse for any rider and I hope you enjoy hearing Angel's story, told by Jacinda. We at Sunnybrook have admired Jacinda's love and commitment to Angel and watched as both of them grew into a wonderful team." Mrs. M smiled at me and Kat gave me thumbs up.

I was beaming. I looked over at Mami, and I could tell she was proud of me.

She was blinking furiously to keep tears from falling.

Mrs. M continued, "I must say, I had my doubts when Jacinda asked if she could take Angel on as a project horse, but she exceeded my expectations and never once needed to ask for help. Jacinda's proven she has what it takes to work with our kids and horses. And above and beyond that, she's shown the love and dedication to work with rescues. Angel's a lucky horse because Jacinda came into her life and saw the good in her when no one else did."

Now everyone was standing and applauding, and it was for *me*. My cheeks were burning and tears tingled in the corners of my eyes. Wow! I couldn't believe it. Kat's mom saying all of those wonderful things about me were the best words I could ever hear. Mrs. M paused and then with a big smile said, "Without further ado, let me introduce Jacinda and Angel."

Again, everyone applauded.

"Come on, Angel, it's our turn," I said as I took the lead line from Kat. We walked into the arena, Angel's bells jingling and her streamers floating behind. I could hear people oohing and aahing.

Mrs. M handed me the microphone. Mrs. M expected me to only introduce Em and Kat and talk a little about how much they'd also *worked* with Angel. But I had way more than that in store. Ha.

Please make this work, please, please. I cleared my throat and gulped. My whole body was shaking as I raised the mic closer to my lips. "Angel's a special horse, which you will soon see. She's not only beautiful, but she comes from a historical background. As Mrs. M said, Angel is an

American Curly horse, which is a special breed that once ran free on the Western Plains. When she first came to Sunnybrook as a rescue, she was in bad shape, and we, um, didn't even know what kind of horse she was. She was matted, dirty and very skinny." I ran my hand down Angel's side. It kind of felt bad to let her hear me talking about her like that, even though I knew she couldn't understand.

I took in another deep breath to calm my frantic heart. "Um, American Curly horses are a special breed because of their curly coats, manes, and fetlocks. Most of all, they have beautiful eyes and curly eyelashes. They are hearty and, um, were very special to the Native Americans and were their favorite mounts." I snatched more air. I wasn't a huge fan of speaking in front of people, but I couldn't wait to unleash our surprise. I can be brave like Em. Do it! Speak. This is the absolute best part! "Emily researched a tattoo I found in her ear, and we discovered Angel was bought from an auction by a circus. And, guess what? She can do tricks! Watch and be amazed by the lovely and spectacular Angel." I took my lunge whip and tapped her on her withers and Angel gave a bow.

The audience cheered.

When she straightened back up, I asked her a question. "Angel, do you like being here?"

She nodded her head "yes".

"Are you an awesome horse?"

She nodded again.

People laughed and I beamed. I could hear the Angels cheering and clapping, and I looked over at my mom and sister. They were cheering too. "Now I want you to really see how special Angel is and why we think she'd make the perfect therapy horse for kids at Sunnybrook." Yeah, gotta stress that. "Here are my assistants, Em and Kat."

The audience clapped for them.

I signaled to Kat and Emily. They moved towards Angel and me. Mrs. M's eyebrow lifted when I looked at her, biting my lip. Yep, the jig was up. She was no dummy. But before she could ask or put a stop to this, Kat and Em were already at my side.

Emily reached up and stroked Angel's side. Kat took the lunge whip and tapped Angel's rump and Angel dropped to the ground. In one swift move, Em bent over, pulled herself up from the wheelchair, grabbed the saddle horn, and swung her other leg over Angel's back and dropped onto the saddle. Kat and I quickly checked to make sure her boots were properly in the stirrups. I heard a gasp of disbelief from the audience, and I looked at Em's mom who had her hand over her mouth. Tears were running down her cheeks. Her dad stared in shock. Em had kept this a secret. It was hard, but she wanted to surprise them.

I backed up a bit, to stand at the ready to help Em if needed, even though I knew she and Angel would rock this. I just wanted to calm Mrs. M to keep her from stopping us.

"Stand, Angel," Kat and Emily said in unison, and Angel stood up effortlessly with Em high on her back.

"Ha ha." Emily picked up the reins, and she was smiling so big I thought her face would break. Emily waved at everyone, clucked and said, "Walk, Angel."

Just to be on the safe side, Kat and I walked on either side of Emily. We weren't exactly side walkers. We were more like … guardian angels.

Angel walked around the ring, bells tinkling. The audience cheered.

Em's mom was jumping up and down and blowing two-hand kisses and her dad was clapping.

Mrs. M's eyes were like saucers, and I had no clue what she was thinking. Was her expression anger or joy that was ready to blast out like a volcano?

A news photographer clicked away, snapping pictures as fast as he could.

Mr. M had just entered the arena to listen to me talk about Angel. He gave me a high five when Kat and I passed him, walking alongside Angel.

Emily was sitting proud as a peacock, riding Angel all by herself. And the icing on the cake! A couple of the wheelchair kids were pushed in with the huge banner we made. It was decorated with handprints, signatures and one footprint. Instead of hanging it, we thought this would be way cooler for them to show it off.

We love you, Mrs. M. Thank you for having such a big… we drew in a big red heart.

She lost it, sobbing into her fist. I hope she knows how much she's truly appreciated. And I also hope she'll open that big heart and keep Angel.

I gotta say, this is the very best day of my life!

As I stood in the gazebo ready to sing and looked out at the crowd, I swear my heart was gonna explode. My throat felt like it had been scraped with sandpaper, and my fingers were frozen on my guitar.

Mr. M adjusted the guitar mic and signaled for me to test it. I swallowed hard and strummed. Kat gave me a thumbs up.

I really hoped I'd only have to sing in front of a few peeps. Nope. Not happenin'. At least a hundred were here to watch me perform. At *least*. A hundred plus people would hear me bomb. No, don't think that. Be positive. Tia was next to Kat with her hands clasped together and she was jumping up and down, so excited to hear me sing. I guess the little imp wasn't such an evil creature after all. Whipping down to pick up my water bottle beside my sneaker because the lump and dry feeling was still assaulting my throat, I bashed my head on the shorter mic, sending a loud "dooosh" through the air. "Oops. Sorry," I said with a cringe and a finger wiggle. "One second."

I snatched my bottle with my hand that was quaking and tingling. I turned away from the crowd to take a few sips and take some deep breaths. *Okay, okay. You can do this. Be strong.*

I set the bottle back down, careful not to crash the microphone this time and stood up straight like Papi said. He was here too, and he waved at me. I almost cried because he looked so proud. He was standing by people and pointing to me to let them know I was his daughter. I winked at him.

So many people were urging me on with their big

smiles. I can do this for them. I can do this for Em, who's smiling ear to ear, trusting that I can do this.

I cleared my throat, closed my eyes, and said, "I wrote this song with my friend, Leese, for all the kids here and for anyone else who feels bullied or forgotten." I could barely get my words out. How on earth was I gonna sing? I started the delicate, soft plucking of my intro that sounded like I might be singing a lullaby, but I picked up the tempo just a hair, right before I started in on my first verse. Suddenly, with determination to prove I could do this, I found my voice and began. "*When you look at me, all you see is the outside. But there's so much more to me than what you can see.*" I dared to open my eyes now.

Kat was signaling me with her thumb to sing louder, and I gave more energy and volume to the chorus.

"*I cry when I'm broken. I sigh when I'm so moved. I sing when I'm lifted into the sky.*"

There was a brief pause, and by the time I got to, "*I crash when I'm so tired,*" smiles on faces were melting. Were people hating this? I froze for a second in my panic, but carried on for Em. "*I hide when I'm terrified. I don't thiiiiiiink, you realize the depths of me. If you did ... if you'd stop to look, then you'd see ... that I'm just like you... I'm just like you-ou-ou. Just like you.*"

Okay, not ugly. People were screaming in excitement and hooting and clapping by the time I got to the second '*just like you*'. I think they were actually digging it.

I looked at Em when I started the next verse and a film was spreading across my eyes, but I couldn't do anything about it. If tears fell, they fell. I couldn't stop now. "*When*

*you pass me by ... you think ... I don't even know. But
you just crushed my heart ... and tore me in two.*"

Emily bent her head and cried into her fist, and the
tears I was trying to hold back made lines on my face like
tiny fairies wanted to add some sparkle to my face.

From what I could hear, the second chorus sounded
smooth as glass to me because I was finding my ground,
despite trying not to choke up too much. It came out more
assertive, more urgent.

For my third verse, I sang, "*When you say those words,
all you do is cut me down. But you don't know my tale.
You just ruined the end.*" I'm not sure if the crowd even
heard my third round of the chorus because they were
cheering so loudly. I finished strong and tacked on several
more, just-like-yous." I did them wavy and soulful and
held the last note out soft and long. Because sometimes a
quiet voice can be more cutting. As I held out that last soft
note, I shot my gaze to Tory and Posh and neither was
looking at me. They both had wet faces that they were
smearing with their fingers.

I scanned the crowd. So many people had big smiles
and shiny eyes. I moved them. I did. Little old me, well ...
big old me. But still, *I* did that. My song made a difference.
Mission accomplished! Yes! This was what being an Angel
was all about. I slid my guitar strap over my head and left
the guitar leaning against the gazebo. I made my way to
my friends, sister and mother. They all hugged me. Mami
pulled my head closer and kissed me on my brow. She said
how proud she was of me. And I lost it. I just started
crying because it was such an amazing experience.

Surprising Emily. Overcoming my fear. Showing the world what I can do. Well, it wasn't the world, but it was a pretty good start. Papi came over to hug me and congratulate me too. I kissed his wet cheek. People I didn't know surrounded me to tell me what a great job I did and told me I should put the song up on iTunes because it was *that* good. When I told them it was for sale at the Angels Club tent for $5, they couldn't leave me fast enough to go pick up a copy. That made me feel a diva.

Well, we had to get back to our booth. When we returned, people recognized us from the arena and that got us more sales in the afternoon.

I passed up spending my money on food and instead bought the most amazing wooden horse carvings ever to go above the doors in my room. I didn't think I'd find anything like that anywhere else, especially not that cheap. I'd put all my birthday money into our club's fund so we could get more supplies for our own fundraiser, so I just said no to the three posters I spotted and wanted. I can get some like that pretty much at any show or even online. But Tia ratted me out to Mami, and she bought the posters and surprised me. I felt bad she spent more money on me, but she said I deserved it.

After 2:30, Kat, Tia and I manned the table for the rest of the day so the other girls could walk around and look at everything and buy stuff if they wanted. It was a fun, fun day, working our booth and telling people about what our Angels Club was all about. Some people didn't even buy anything, they just donated money. They became our special angels.

When Kat left to go help her mom encourage kids who were nervous about signing up for therapy, River, this thirteen-year-old Cherokee boy who volunteers here, came up to our booth. He knocked on the table and picked up one of Tia's horse pictures.

"I made that," Tia chirped.

"Excellent craftsmanship," he said. "I'll take the blue one. My gram'll love it." After Tia took the five dollar bill from him, smiling big at the compliment, he said, "Where's Trouble?"

"Not here," I said with a glare because he always called Kat *Trouble*, even though he was a good dose of trouble himself. They were both spirited and stubborn, so they fought constantly, like I'm talking major blowout arguments. "Kat's helping her mom, so she's not here for you to bug. Shoo."

"Goodie." He shook his floppy black hair. "I wasn't actually lookin' for Kat. I wanted to talk to you privately."

"I can keep secrets," Tia insisted with a hop and her fingers laced together.

"Yeah right." I cracked up because that was the biggest fib I'd ever heard.

"I can!"

"Whatever. Talk about what?" I said.

"Mrs. M said you're the one to talk to about, um, joining the club."

"Uh, yeah … I guess I'd be the one." I cringed though. Letting him in would be a very, very bad thing. I just don't know if letting more people in at this point would be a good thing, not until we can learn to avoid fights. Even the Heavenly Seven had its moments of hellion spirit and fire *without* the added pressure of boys, especially *this* one. "For real?" I asked, assuming he was joking. "You really want to join?"

"Definitely," he said. "It's a good cause."

"Are you just being snarky or are you serious?"

"Nope, no snark, not today. I'm really serious."

"I'll have to let you know once we put it to a vote."

"All right. Good. You know where to find me."

I puffed air at the ridiculousness of that as he walked away with his blue horse picture.

Tia could probably tell what I was thinking by my sneer. "You're not even gonna tell them about him wanting to join, are you."

"Nope. *Nada.* He doesn't get along with Kat, like, at all. That'd be willingly pulling a hornet's nest in our club."

She shrugged. "Well, he was nice to me. I think we should vote on it."

"Maybe. I'll think about it." But I didn't really think about. We were too busy cleaning up our booth after a long day.

We went into Kat's house for lemonade and to count our money. After giving Mrs. M her spot money back, our coinage and bills tallied up to $753, including bake sale money, donations and sales of my demo, which sold out! Oh my goodness! We screamed in excitement.

"What! That's like insane," Kat said.

"That's way more than I expected we'd get," Posh said, sitting on Kat's bed, next to Em, who was laying on her side, propped up on her elbow because it was a long, tiring day for her.

"I know. Me too," I said. "Our horseshoes were a really big hit. We only have 8 left. Thank you so so much for thinking of it, Posh. I really liked how they all came out."

"Me too. People were even excited to get my free pinwheels," Em said. "My mom helped me cut them, and I'm so glad we got them done for the event. Thanks for putting me into your song, Jacinda. That was so sweet. And with just a few words, it was so powerful."

"No problem. As I was writing it, I couldn't *not* do it."

"The pinwheels were really a great idea," Tory rushed out. "The kids I gave them to were so thrilled." I couldn't help but think that she was flipping the subject to get out from under the heat of the spotlight of judgment. She can irritate me with her perfectionist ways and abruptness, but I was no longer mad at her. She didn't need to feel guilty anymore. That was all in the past. It was a new day. She's a better human being now. Although it makes my tongue feel pasty to say it, I considered her a true friend. Sometimes friends just have rough edges or things you don't like, but that doesn't mean you can't be or aren't friends. It just means she and I have to work a bit harder to overcome our differences to stay connected. But I like challenges. Tory started to cry. "I'm so sorry, Jacinda."

I hugged her and said in her ear, "I know. You already apologized. It's okay. We're friends now. I didn't think it would happen, but we are. I forgive you. And all the stings are gone."

"You mean that?" When I nodded, she hugged me back.

"Thank you, thank you. I don't deserve your friendship or forgiveness."

"Well, Mami always says, going through life holding onto grudges just makes you ugly inside. It's not worth it. I'd rather feel warm-hearted and free. Wouldn't you?"

"Yep."

"Yeah, I guess we're kinda friends too," Leese said to her with a shrug, her thumbs in her front jean pockets. "You're not so bad ... when you're not being bossy."

"Thanks," Tory said and then she laughed. "I consider all of you my friends, even you, Leese. I'll try to be nicer and not so demanding, okay, guys?"

"Yeah right," Posh said.

"Ahh, but we love you anyway," Kat said. "I also have too much awesomeness for people to handle. People just don't understand those of us with big mouths and personalities."

"Oh my gosh!" Posh drew out the "o" in gosh like a note. "Can't believe we have *seven-hundred and fifty-three dollars*! Wooooo!"

We repeated the amount in screams, again and again, jumping up and down.

Emily raised her fists to jump in her own way and cracked up, probably because of how silly and wild we looked, going all chimp crazy. "There's so much we can do with that money," she said. "So many people we can help."

"I know. The world won't know what hit it," I said.

When we were done making a new list of Angels' kisses to hand out and reading the needs that had come into the

Need Box, we went downstairs, washed our hands, and started making sandwiches.

Mrs. M came in and rested her hand on the counter and wiped her brow, surely exhausted after a long day's work. "You girls were all magnificent today. I'm so proud of you. The fundraiser was a huge success. It blew my mind. I didn't expect such generosity. We pulled in so many sponsors." As I took my first bite, she added, "We even ... got five offers for Angel."

I froze with my mouth full, terrified to move. I'm pretty sure the kitchen started melting just like in that melting clocks painting I once saw by that artist I can't remember at the moment because all I feel is a sharp pain in my chest. Okay, the room started spinning too. *Ugh, I think I'm gonna be sick, once I find my stomach again.*

"And guess what?" Mrs. M said. "Angel has a home now! A real home. The girl who craved to have her more than anyone, beat everyone else out. The twenty-two *thousand* Sunnybrook will get is just blowing my mind right now. I can't even believe it!"

No, no, no. This couldn't be happening. No one craves Angel more than me! I was still choking on sandwich, forcing it down with a swallow that felt like I'd taken in glass instead of bread and thinly sliced roast beef. When my throat was finally clear, I muttered, "That's ... so great," but enthusiasm was not there. *Sand* could've said that more convincingly than I just did.

"Wow. Angel was sold for twenty-two grand?" Kat said. "That's so cool!" Kat was clouded by dollar signs at first, but then realized in a flash how monstrously huge the cost was. Her eyes went wet at the brutal realization of loss when she looked at me. "I mean... um, I'm sure she'll enjoy her new home."

I zipped my gaze away so I wouldn't dissolve into a puddle of sorrow.

"Well, you girls know how special she is," Mrs. M said.

I couldn't contain my heartbreak anymore and lost it. Of course I know! That's why I worked so hard to try to keep her here. I started crying.

Mrs. M stroked my head as she said, "Now, Jacinda, if you're gonna be working with rescues, you need to learn not to get too attached. Often times, you're working with a horse that's just in your care temporarily."

"I know," I said, sobs bubbling out. "I know that. I just ... love her so much."

"But not *this* time."

"What," I said, shaking my head, confused.

"I got some offers for sale, but the signups to *sponsor* Angel, not even just pledges, but people paying right on the spot, far exceeded any bid for sale. Others recognize her value in therapy as well."

"So, does that mean she's staying at Sunnybrook?" I asked, with rays of sun streaming down on me suddenly. I had a whoosh of hope.

"Unless you want to trailer her in on weekends."

"What do you mean *me?*"

"She's *your* horse. You decide."

"Like, my project still."

"No, I mean, Sunnybrook Farm is giving her to you. So you can decide where she lives, but she will need to be used in therapy for us to keep all the sponsorship money."

"Is this some kinda joke?"

"No, honey. It's very evident how much you love her and how excellent of a job you've done. I just don't have the heart to sell her to anyone outside of our big, happy family."

Tears streamed down my face. "You mean it? She's *mine* mine. Like, my *own* horse? Angel, who I love so so much, more than any horse ever? She's mine?"

"That's exactly what I mean?"

"And I can stable her here?"

"As long as she's in the program, she has a home here."

"Oh my goodness! Thank you, thank you, thank you, Mrs. M! I don't even know what to say. This is the nicest thing anybody has ever done for me?"

"Yay!" Emily cried. "Angel can stay! She'll be so excited when we tell her."

As I hugged Mrs. M, I broke down and cried in unequaled happiness. "I'm really sorry we snuck behind your back Mrs. M. I know it was wrong, I just wanted to surprise you so badly and show you how great Angel would be in therapy."

"Let me be clear, I'm not at all happy about that. The next time you girls want to show me something about a horse or a child, don't do it on the sly. That's extremely dangerous. I can't have you girls taking risks with the animals or the students. Understand? If something happened, we could get sued. This is no joke, nothing to play around with."

"Yes, I know. I'm so so sorry," I said. "It won't happen again. I'll act more responsibly, I swear."

"Me too," Kat said. "Sorry, Mom."

"Well, *I'm* not," Emily said with an arm cross of stubbornness. "Nope. Not sorry."

We all cracked up.

This was the best day ever! Emily rocked it. Angel rocked it. I rocked it. The Angels made a ton of money and worked well together. And Angel can not only stay at Sunnybrook helping kids in therapy, but she's *mine*, all mine, my very own horse.

There's nothing in the whole wide world that can bring me down now. I have everything I want. Life is totally, absolutely perfect!

22

I loved being a horse owner. I still couldn't believe I had my very own horse. And I loved being a good-deed-giving Angel, even though it wasn't totally headache free.

The two weeks following the show were crazy-hectic for the Club as we were moving towards the holidays and had more funds to operate with now.

We began handing out Angels' kisses like penny candy. And, um, I was just gonna say the *town* was inspired, but really, people all over the state, thanks to the photos and great write-up on the front page of the paper, were also reaching out and doing good deeds.

See? I knew spreading just a little bit of good cheer around like fairy dust would grow and move like wildfire. More people wanted to join our club, and I had to practically beat them off with a stick. We were compiling a list of possible new members. But I told River, "No way," even though I hadn't even brought it to a vote. I just want us settled down before we start adding new faces and feisty personalities into the mix.

Emily was proving to be an excellent and much-needed diffuser, like those experts who deactivate bombs just seconds before the big BOOM, because arguments were still whirling up like tornadoes here and there, and in the same way, touching down in the middle of us out of nowhere, threatening to wreck everything. But we *were* getting better I think, learning how not to tick each other off and instead putting Emily's words and ideas into action. We're *trying* to work harder, to be the true angels we're supposed to be.

We did have an email address that Emily set up, but we kept it generally private. It was mostly for communicating with vendors and learning about other horse and craft shows we could sell at this winter. But it seemed to be getting around and landing in the hands of people who really wanted to get in touch with us. I received another reply from Angel's previous owner who was in assisted living now. I sent him some pics of her from the showcase in all her ribbons and a note, and since then, we've chatted back and forth about Angel, who he called Star Burst. He cried to know she was happy and helping people and that her sweet nature was being appreciated.

I smiled reading the thank you notes we got.

I got laid off two days before I got your note that said, 'Life is full of ups and downs. Keep your chin up during the downs, so you don't miss any of the ups coming your way.' That little bit of encouragement cheered me up in a dark hour and place. I still haven't found a job, but I'm more optimistic, all thanks to you. Keep up the good work, Angels.

I personally wrote that note. It was inspired by Papi's words of wisdom to me to always look up. I'm glad it ended up with someone who needed exactly those words, since we handed them out randomly. I read some more notes of thanks and they made me cry. I would read all these at our next brunch meeting at Kat's house later today when she gets back from church.

I then went into my own inbox and flicked my tongue when I saw a message from the Curly Registry. Well, finally! It took them long enough! Only like, *weeks.* Kat and Em, and maybe Mrs. M too, will be so excited when I can tell them more of the deets about Angel's past. I had a sick feeling in the pit of my stomach though. Hopefully, she didn't suffer anything worse than being neglected or getting ditched by the circus that raised her. It would just break my heart to know my beautiful Angel had been abused or mistreated or whatever.

Dear Miss Gonzalez, Thank you for writing us and sending us information about your project horse. Based on the appearance, age and special mark on her rump, we are certain this is the mare that was reported stolen by her owner, Krista Belcher, five years ago, when she was an eight-month-old filly. Please contact Ms. Belcher as soon as possible so she can make arrangements to pick up her horse. Thank you again. And have a great day.

– Linda Day, American Bashkir Curly Registry

Krista's contact information was at the bottom. It *was* worse. The sick feeling in my stomach spiked and my chest instantly ached like a heavy rock slammed into it from across the room.

Stolen? No ... she's my horse, my horse. MINE. This Krista doesn't even know her anymore. Not like I do. She's mine. Mrs. M gave her to me, and I trained her, I take care of her, I love her. This can't be happening. My lip quivered and eyes went ablaze before they spilled lava down my cheeks. "I don't want to lose you, Angel. I can't."

I skipped breakfast and ran for the door in a rush to see Angel.

"What's wrong, *mija*?" Mami said.

"*Nada*. Gotta work," was all I could spit out. I was already sobbing my heart and lungs out when I hopped on my bike and zipped to Sunnybrook. It didn't feel so sunny today. A knife felt like it was sticking out of my chest, and this loud, threatening rumble in my head swore lightning was about to zap away my happiness. I bit my lip so no one would hear my sobs.

Angel had her head poking out over her stall when I dashed into her barn. She put her head down to meet mine when she heard me crying. I opened the gate and walked into her stall. I clutched her around the neck. My body was gonna burst from sorrow. It felt so close to exploding and I shuddered uncontrollably. I had shivers and pain all over. "I can't lose you, Angel. See how sweet you are, pretty girl? You love to comfort people. You're a perfect therapy horse now. You're so happy here, doing what you love. And you're mine. *My* horse. No, no, no. No one could love you as much as I do." She rubbed her nose on my head as I hugged her tighter and refused to let go.

Why'd I ever contact that dumb registry in the first place? Angel's *our* horse and what about Emily? She loves Angel so much, and she's her special riding horse now. It'll break her heart as much as mine. And what about the other kids in therapy who can't mount? They've been just sitting on Angel as she sweetly lies on the ground and hugging her. She's given those kids so much love and something to strive for. Everyone adores her to pieces, including Kat, who still affectionately refers to her as Rat Face most of the time, but at least I know she truly loves her. And the worst rotten cherry of all, besides my heart being totally shattered into a million sharp bits, is Mrs. M will also be out *all* that sponsorship money. No, I can't let her go. I can't.

I took a step back and said, "You know what? It's okay. I have a plan. It'll be okay. I don't *have* to tell anyone, and I won't." I wiped my face and took a deep breath, certain of my decision. "Neither this Krista Belcher person nor the registry knows where you are, so no one at Sunnybrook even has to find out about this. No one even knows I contacted the registry. I'll keep this our secret."

Angel bobbed her head up and down, saying yes to me, like she really understood what she was agreeing to.

I ran my fingers over the soft ringlets of her mane, while looking into her eyes. "Even your sweet gaze says you know who you belong to. You know you're mine and how much I love you. That's it. I'm definitely keeping you. It'll be okay." I put her halter on, clipped the lead line to it, and then walked her out to the round pen to work on the new tricks I was trying to teach her. I stayed as long as

I could and tried not to think about this horrible nightmare that had just crashed down on me right when everything was so perfectly perfect.

For two weeks, I could hardly eat. Mami could tell something was bothering me and kept asking me about it. Even the Angels could tell I wasn't my usual chipper self. Although guilt was starting to gnaw at my stomach, I refused to open any more emails from that Krista Belcher, and she sent at least four.

But the more time I had to think about it, the more it hit me like a slap that as much as I love Angel, how can I be an Angel if I can't do the right thing? How would *I* feel if someone stole her from me and wouldn't give her back? It would break my heart. I needed to tell someone, so I caved and phoned Kat and Emily and asked them to meet me at the barn. This was an absolute emergency!

I was shaking and close to tears when I met Kat inside.

"What's wrong, Jacinda? You look like a wreck," Kat said in her usual snarky way.

I turned my face when I heard Emily clomping in the door with her crutches. Her mom dropped her off. She was using the crutches rather than the wheelchair, more and more, and said eventually she'll chuck 'em in the trash, and I totally believe it.

"Em, we're in here," I shouted and didn't move to meet her. I didn't know how I was going to tell them the bad news, especially Emily. Losing Angel will break her heart as much as mine. No one was in the barn but the three of us. It was very quiet, so still, except for the few horses munching hay in their stalls.

"What's up?" Em asked. "You're freaking me out. You're not moving, are you? Why all the secrecy?"

Kat said, "Yeah, spit it out. You're acting so weird."

I sniffled, to hold back some sobs. But tears rolled down my cheeks when I started to explain. "I was trying to find out on my own where Angel came from before the circus, so I could surprise and impress you."

"Yeah, so?" Kat spat. "What's that gotta do with anything?"

"Uh, it's bad. It's bad news," Emily cried, covering her ears. "I don't wanna know. Don't say it."

I gulped and said, "Yes. It's very, very bad."

"What?" Kat cried. "What bad news?"

I grabbed Em's wrist and said, "You need to hear this, Em." When she nodded and let go of her ears, I continued with my voice breaking up, "I can't keep my mouth shut any longer. A lady, some Krista Belcher person, is Angel's real owner … and … she wants her back."

"Wait, wait, hold on a minute. Who's she and how do you know her?" Kat asked.

I totally lost it and started blubbering the whole wretched tale about how I emailed the Curly Registry weeks before the event to see if they knew anything about Angel and that they finally got back to me and said she was stolen from this Krista lady when she was just a filly.

"Oh no," Emily asked, with tears running down her face and a quivering lip. "We're gonna lose Angel?"

"That's why I called you here," I said, pulling myself together. "What should we do?"

"What do you mean, *do*? You didn't email her back yet?" Kat asked.

"No, I just ... couldn't do it. Why'd I ever contact that registry in the first place. Worst decision ever!"

"Well, now what?" Emily asked. "It'll break Angel's heart."

Kat said, "You *need* to email her back! We have to do the right thing, Jacinda. We're *Angels* now."

"I know, but I didn't wanna do it without telling you first. I hid it at first, but the guilt has been eating me alive. I was kinda hoping you'd talk me out of blabbing the truth ... or something, though I know what I have to do."

"Don't tell," Emily cried, with her fingers laced tightly together. "Please."

"She *has* to tell," Kat said. "It's only right."

"I know, I know," Emily groaned. "But I hate it."

"Me too. I hate it," I said. "Surely she'll wanna come and get her horse."

"I know I'd be there in a New York minute if someone stole Sassy."

"Right. As much as it kills, I absolutely know what I have to do." I struggled to get out the words, "I just hate ... to lose my horse ... my sweet, sweet Angel," because sobs took over.

We cried our eyes out as we hugged Angel. We didn't know exactly what was going to happen next, but one thing was for sure ... we had to tell Mrs. M.

23

My heart felt ripped up and totally broken. No, no. This couldn't be happening! I was losing my horse! My Angel, the horse I love with all my heart.

I emailed Krista Belcher later that day and told her Angel was at Sunnybrook Farm and available for pickup. I explained that she was my project horse and was now being used in a therapeutic riding program and so very happy doing it. I told her how much everyone adores her. I thought she'd email me back and say, "Great job, why don't you keep her." Yeah, that didn't happen. The worst thing imaginable happened, exactly what I feared most. She wanted Angel back.

I let Mrs. M know, and this Krista Belcher lady already contacted Mrs. M and made arrangements to pick her up.

So, I had just two hours to spend with *my* horse and say my final goodbyes. This was so beyond horrible.

Emily, Kat and I were waiting with the McKinleys

when we heard the rumble of the truck coming up the dirt driveway. My stomach bottomed out and Emily started breathing crazy and looking like she was gonna seriously puke, clutching her stomach like she was.

The truck stopped and the driver and a woman stepped out of the cab. Mr. and Mrs. M went to greet them. I heard Mrs. M say, "Why don't you stretch a little and have something to drink? I'll have the girls get Angel tacked, and then they can bring her into the indoor and show you what Angel can do and what an amazing horse she is."

Krista Belcher, a blonde with an eager smile, seemed happy to get out and stretch after the long trip from Pennsylvania where she now had her farm. I pictured her looking like the devil, but she had a very friendly face. The man with her shook Mr. M's hand, and then they walked towards the house. Mrs. M called out to us to get Angel ready and bring her into the indoor riding area.

Emily and I were a slobbery mess of tears as we went to get Angel for the very last time.

"Buck up, cowgirls," Kat said. "Now's the time to show Angel off and what we've done for her. Falling apart'll help no one."

"Yeah." Emily sniffed her tears back. "Hey, I know! What if we just get on horses and ride away with Angel?"

"Emily, we can't," I said, "as much as I'd *like* to do that. We have to be strong. Angel's not actually our horse to keep." I had to show some courage now. After two weeks of crying, I think I can do this. I think. Angel deserved my best and I'm sure this Krista Belcher will love her as much as we do. After all, she was, I mean, *is* her horse.

Mr. and Mrs. M came out of the house with Krista Belcher and the man she came with. We were walking Angel into the indoor and Mrs. M called to us to come meet Angel's real owners.

"Errr, no way. I don't wanna meet them," Em groaned. "They're mean, taking Angel away."

"They're *not* mean," Kat said. "She's Angel's rightful owner. And we can't avoid them. My mom and dad wouldn't like that."

"All right. We can do this. Let's go," I said. "We need to be brave for Angel's sake, so she won't be scared."

"Okay," Emily groaned with a scowl. "I don't want *our* horse to get upset."

I led Angel over there and Kat and Em came with me.

Mrs. M introduced us, but after a brief hello, all that Krista Belcher could do was slobber and fawn over Angel and say how beautiful she was and how much she missed her. I think she was crying, but I couldn't stand to look. As she hugged my favorite girl, I was shocked to feel the love radiating from Krista for my horse.

When she let go, I led Angel into the indoor and everyone followed. Emily and Kat came with me into the ring, while everyone else stood against the wall. I vehemently decided I wasn't going to show them *all* of the tricks Angel could do. That was *our* special thing, especially the new ones I taught her, but Emily will ride. I could tell by their conversation, the McKinleys already filled them in about the program for the kids and how much Angel has already done in such a short time.

Angel stood quietly, waiting for us to tell her what we

wanted. Standing beside her, I gave her the cue to drop down so Emily could mount.

Krista gasped when she saw *my* precious white horse obediently wait for Emily to get into the saddle.

Kat and I made sure her legs were properly in the stirrups. For some reason, today, Em's legs looked smaller and thinner than ever. Emily's sniveling had me so close to cracking myself, but one look at Kat helped me to hold it together. She knew exactly what I was feeling and made a goofy face to get me to laugh.

Angel, on my up-cue, stood and Emily smiled big and waved. All was forgotten when she was in the saddle. She had a job to do and, as always, Emily had made up her mind. She'd show that Krista Belcher that Angel had a perfectly fine job and home already, and it *wasn't* at *her* farm near the Amish! Emily said, "Walk on, Angel," and, of course, Angel moved off.

I couldn't look at Krista Belcher, so I didn't know what her reaction was. I was intently watching Em ride her for the very last time. All the joy Angel brings here'll be gone, gone. I couldn't believe Angel was minutes away from leaving me forever. I wiped tears from my eyes.

Emily walked Angel once around but didn't stop. Next thing I knew, I heard her say, "Trot, Angel." And she did just that and Emily's laughter filled the indoor. I heard everyone clapping and looked over to see Krista Belcher clapping loudest. She was actually cheering.

When Emily finished three more laps, she brought Angel to a halt, and I gave Angel the cue to drop down again. Em dismounted with a slow slide, threw her arms around Angel's neck, and wailed. I was trying so hard to be strong, but I lost it entirely and started crying too.

"I'm gonna miss you, Angel. I don't want you to go. You're my best friend."

I saw Krista wiping tears away, and Mr. M said they were going inside to talk.

We led Angel to her barn to remove her tack. When we had her on the crossties, I lifted the saddle off her for the last time. "Good girl," I said, giving her a cookie. "Love you and I'll miss you. Don't ever forget me. I won't forget you. We're friends forever." I hugged her so tight.

Kat, Em and I gave sweet Angel one last humungous hug and walked her to her stall. My heart was aching like it got punched and pools of liquid sat on the ridges of my eyelids, clouding my vision until they spilled away. We started to leave the barn in tatters, like our wings had been torn off and hearts stomped on.

When I lifted my head, I saw that Krista Belcher walking towards us. "Aw, great." My stomach dropped.

Emily and Kat were, for once, out of words.

As Krista Belcher stood eye-to-eye with me, literally, because I'm as tall as she is, she said, "After watching Emily ride, I realized, *this* is where Angel belongs. It's so sad for me to let her go, especially when I *just* found her, but after everything she's been through, I'd hate to uproot her again when she's clearly so happy and loved here."

What? Did I hear right? Is she talking to me?

Emily dragged me out of my haze of confusion by squealing in delight. "She's staying? You mean it? Yes, yes, yes!" She pumped her fists.

So this wasn't just a dream?

Standing with her mouth open, Kat finally found her voice, "Whaaaat? Are you punking us?"

Krista just smiled, with tears in her eyes. "No, I sincerely mean it. My husband and I both agreed. We want her to be here where she'll be happy and well-taken care of. But ... we do have one condition."

"Awww, yeah, what's that?" Kat asked all leery, crossing her arms.

"That Jacinda stays in touch with me and lets me know how Angel is and sends photos every now and then, *especially* as she's used in therapy. I'm thinking of starting my own program with a friend, and this has inspired me to go for it much sooner."

What! "Oh my goodness!" I got my horse back? Are you kidding me! Awesome, awesome! "Thank you so so much. I'm wicked sorry I thought you were the devil. I was wrong. You're an *Angel* just like us." I hugged her, and then I dashed back to Angel's stall and hugged my beautiful, sweetheart, Angel. Mine!

Krista laughed.

I cried in my elation and jumped up and down. Okay, I take back what I said before. *This* is my best day ever! Angel's mine, truly mine, again and forever, and I'm so psyched she'll get to be here for the kids at Sunnybrook, especially my very good friend, Emily. My heart was flooded with sunshine and roses right now. I couldn't be happier than this very moment! Just not possible.

Oh, by the way. In case you missed it or couldn't tell... *horses* are my passion. I love, love, LOVE them!

Thanks for reading, Cuties!!!

Learn more about the authors, merchandise and the *Angels Club* series at www.angelsclubkids.com and www.facebook.com/angelsclubnovel.

Don't miss Kat and River's story in

Angels Club 2: THE TROUBLE WITH BOYS

ABOUT THE AUTHORS

 **COURTNEY VAIL** In addition to writing quirky, twisty books for teens and adults, Courtney works from home as a graphic designer and book formatter. She's married to a *should-be*-famous comedian and has three kids who make her house LOUD and messy and do things like turn her veggie garden into Jurassic Park, but she thoroughly loves her life. She's a member of Authors Selling Books in Western Mass. Courtney is a *major* sports junky and loves to run, visit amusement parks (and ride all the roller coasters first), skate, cook, and watch standup or anything that cracks her up or makes her heart race or neck tingle. *Angels Club* is her first novel for kids.

SANDRA J. HOWELL is an avid horse enthusiast and was the first breeder in Massachusetts of the rare American Bashkir Curly horse. Her lifelong passion for Curly horses led her to write two Equine novels, *Spirit of a Rare Breed* and *Saving GiGi*. Howell, a college professor, has been a contributing writer, featuring the American Bashkir Curly horse, for Equine journals and magazines. She has been featured on television, radio talk shows and news media, and has received numerous letters from  Native Americans thanking her for promoting and advocating for their favored steed. Howell is a founding member of Authors Selling Books of Western Mass and is a member of the Independent Publishers of New England. Her novels are showcased at the *New England Equine Affaire* and promoted through many Equine organizations.

CPSIA information can be obtained
at www.ICGtesting.com
Printed in the USA
FFOW03n0956050617
36305FF